BLOOD AND GOLD

BLOOD AND GOLD

TODHUNTER BALLARD

WHEELER
CHIVERS

This Large Print edition is published by Wheeler Publishing, Waterville, Maine, USA and by BBC Audiobooks Ltd, Bath, England.
Wheeler Publishing, a part of Gale, Cengage Learning.

LIBRARY OF CONGRESS CATALOGING-IN-PUBLICATION DATA

Ballard, Todhunter, 1903–
  [Gopher gold]
  Blood and gold / by Todhunter Ballard.
    p. cm. — (Wheeler Publishing large print western)
  Previously published as: Gopher gold.
  ISBN-13: 978-1-59722-691-2 (pbk. : alk. paper)
  ISBN-10: 1-59722-691-2 (pbk. : alk. paper)
  1. Large type books. I. Title.
  PS3503.A5575B56 2008
  813'.54—dc22   2007044815

BRITISH LIBRARY CATALOGUING-IN-PUBLICATION DATA AVAILABLE

Published in 2008 in the U.S. by arrangement with Golden West Literary Agency.
Published in 2008 in the U.K. by arrangement with Golden West Literary Agency.
U.K. Hardcover: 978 1 405 64412 9 (Chivers Large Print)
U.K. Softcover: 978 1 405 64413 6 (Camden Large Print)

Printed in the United States of America
1 2 3 4 5 6 7 12 11 10 09 08

BLOOD AND GOLD

CHAPTER ONE

It was after midnight when the news of the epidemic reached Goldfield, but the tidings spread through the camp like a grass fire before a driving wind.

Doctor Adam Patch was far from the first to hear it. He was playing poker with Tex Rickard, Kid Highley and three mineowners in Tex's Northern Saloon. He was losing, which was uncommon, for Patch was reputedly as great a gambler as he was a surgeon.

He was a big man, his body lean and hard, showing no hint of fat. His hands were large and strong and moved with confidence, their natural aptitude heightened by careful training with both cards and the knife.

Poker played properly requires deep concentration, and the men at the table were oblivious to the wave of silence as it washed down the length of the long, smoky room. The three roulette wheels stopped spinning first. The dice ceased to clatter across the green cloth. Then the faro banks were quiet. Even the twelve bartenders behind the sixty-foot counter suddenly had nothing to do.

The desert country had known sickness before, and was weary of it. Only four years ago the fever had nearly depopulated Tonopah. Men had died there like flies and left behind a wholesome fear of the disease.

But the game at the rear table progressed, its players unaware of the word of tragedy just brought out of the barren hills. Not until Wyatt Earp moved back and paused at Rickard's elbow did the saloon man look up from the bunched cards held closely in his cupped hands to raise an inquiring eyebrow.

"Trouble?"

Earp was pit boss for the night, an old hand around the gaming tables, but even his stoic calm was a little ruffled at the moment.

"Indian Jake just came in from Gopher. They've got the fever up there, bad."

Tex Rickard laid his cards face down, slowly. Adam Patch was listening with close attention.

"How bad?"

Wyatt Earp shrugged. The drooping mustache, already touched with gray, gave to his face a totally false appearance of ineffectuality.

"I don't know. Jake is up at Mary Collins'. I guess he's in pretty bad shape. Some teamsters found him a few miles out on the Tonopah road."

He turned, having told them all he knew, and went back to his high stool in the center of the pit. From this vantage point he could watch the play at all the games. But there was no longer any play to watch. The men had formed into small groups, those who had already been through the fever relating their experiences in low voices.

Adam Patch stood up deliberately. He moved with an athlete's grace, a striking figure in his long, square-tailed coat and soft, wide-brimmed hat. He turned without speaking, leaving his companions to debate the news behind him. His sure step carried him around the groups along the bar with the rhythm of a trained dancer navigating a crowded ballroom, to reach the door quickly.

Outside, the main street was as crowded as usual, for this camp never slept. A dozen men hailed him as he passed, for there was no better known citizen in Goldfield than Adam Patch.

The Collins' house for all its smallness

had the air of being lived in well. He crossed the sunbaked yard and climbed the two steps to the shallow porch and knocked, hearing the woman's steps as she moved across the inner room.

"Who is it?"

"Adam Patch."

She drew the bolt and opened the door, saying as she stood aside,

"Come in, Doctor. I was going to call you but I haven't dared to leave him yet."

Patch went inside, closing the door and looking at Mary Collins. She was twenty-four, tall for a woman, high breasted with a proud carriage that made men turn to stare at her on the street.

Her hair was fair, and he was surprised at the deep, quiet serenity mirrored in her gray eyes as they met his. He felt an unwilling stir at the wordless pull of her presence.

He knew her as he knew a thousand other people in this roaring town, to speak to on the street, to smile pleasantly at when they met in a store, nothing more. He looked carefully away.

The room in which they stood was too small, but the rough board walls had been covered with printed cloth. The carpet was worn thin but it was clean, and the small organ with its yellowed keys lent the place an air of richness and of peace.

He had the moment only to look around, then she was leading him into the tiny bedroom at the rear, and he was gazing down at the thin face of the old man on the bed.

Indian Jake was not an Indian at all. Rather he was a squaw man who had lived most of his life among his wife's people. His hair was shoulder length, black and greasy, and Patch knew that it was not worn long for beauty's sake but to conceal the fact that Jake had no ears.

Jake Longstreet was a character throughout the country. Related to the old General, he had come west directly after the war. In Austin he had joined a gang of stage robbers, and when the vigilance committee finally caught up with them he had been spared because of his youth.

Instead of hanging him with the others, the committee had shaved off his ears as a warning to honest men that he was a criminal. It was a mistake they did not live to repeat, for story had it that Jake had hunted them down one after the other with the patience of a stalking wolf, and had not rested until the last vigilante had died before his smoking gun.

Then he had vanished, living with the

11

Indians for a good ten years until at length he settled on a little hay ranch in Belmont Valley.

The silver strike at Tonopah, the following find at Goldfield, had brought him back into the world, and no one bothered to revive the old charges, since at eighty he could still draw a gun faster than most men.

Like an animal he seemed to sense that Patch was watching him, and twisted in the blankets. His thin old body was gaunt to the point that the bones seemed to push outward against the leathery skin. His eyes opened, sharp and black as they had been on that day when he had lost his ears, and his voice was surprisingly strong.

"Hi, Doc. Did you get my message?"

"What message, Jake? I got no message, but I heard in the Northern that there's sickness at Gopher."

"That there is," said the old man. "Funny sickness, Doc, like the stuff they had at Tonopah four, five years back. You're talking to a man on the street and an hour later you hear he's dead."

"The fever?"

"Yeah, the fever. They turn black."

"How do you feel?"

The blue rind of his lips parted to show the stumps of half a dozen snaggle teeth.

12

"Me? I'm all right. Takes more than a fever to kill old Jake. I just walked myself to death, that's all. I'll be okay tomorrow."

"Sure you will," said Patch. He reached out and laid a finger on the old man's wrist. The pulse was even, strong and normal, giving mute testimony that the heart which beat in the sunken breast was functioning perfectly. And there was no sign of temperature. "Can you tell me about it?"

"What's there to tell?" Jake sounded impatient, with the waspishness of the old. "They've got the sickness. Doc Trumble, he took care of them while he could, then a week ago he died, and there's no one left to care for the sick ones."

"How many men are left in camp?"

"Maybe a hundred on their feet when I started."

"Why don't they leave?"

Jake's grin came again as if he thoroughly enjoyed his joke. "They don't want to leave the gold ball."

"What gold ball?"

"Ain't you heard? Clint Collins and Sam Dohne took out a lot of gold on the first strike. Some say there's maybe half a million dollars' worth. And she's a wild camp. I thought I'd seen some wild ones in my day, but they was nothing like Gopher. The boys used to say that at Bodie they had a man for breakfast every day. Well, in Gopher they got one for breakfast, lunch and dinner."

He stopped, gathering strength, then went on.

"So every tough in town sat around waiting for them to try to ship that gold out and planning to hold up the wagon. But Sam's a smartie. What'd he do? He cast it in a single solid ball. It weighs something more than a ton. And he set it on his porch. He figured no holdup man would have any way of handling it even if they stole it."

Patch had to grin. Like all of Goldfield, he appreciated a good joke. Then he sobered.

"What's that got to do with the sickness?"

"Hold your horses. I'm coming to that. No one is going to leave Gopher as long as that ball sets there. Everybody figures maybe the whole town will die off and leave him with the gold for himself."

Adam Patch was not surprised. He had grown up in the gold camps and he knew that the lure of the yellow metal would make men forget danger and reason, and take impossible risks.

"Why doesn't Sam haul the thing out?"

A dry cackle shook Jake's chest. "They

can't. They cast it last fall, and just as they were about to leave, a flash flood hit us. It took out fifty miles of road. I mean it really washed it out. You couldn't get over it with a horse, let alone a wagon.

"Then the snow came and we were snowbound for weeks. Now it's melting, and the fever's hit. I tell you, Doc, the whole thing is a mess." He sighed. He was asleep before Patch realized it.

Slowly Adam turned back into the front room to find Mary Collins waiting for him. She said without preamble,

"I heard. Are you going to Gopher?"

"Someone has to."

"I'm going with you."

He shook his head. "Have you any idea what that country is like in the winter?"

"My husband's there."

"And the fever. There's no need to expose you to that."

"What is it?"

Again he shook his head. "We don't know. The doctors never agreed on what the outbreak was at Tonopah. We only know that it emptied the camp within two weeks. Those who could, ran. Of those who couldn't, over fifty per cent died."

"How soon will you leave?"

"As soon as possible. But no woman

15

should try to go."

"If you won't take me I'll go alone, or have Jake take me. He'll do anything I tell him to."

Adam Patch shrugged. Above all things he was a gambler, and despite his medical training he was something of a fatalist.

"Be ready at four," he said, and turned out of the house.

CHAPTER TWO

From almost the moment when Adam Patch's first resentful cry rang down the frosty air of Gold Canyon, high on the barren slope of Mount Davidson, he was destined to study medicine.

It was not a decision that the red, wrinkled infant made for himself. The decision was made by the Chief.

James Patrick Patch was a man of enormous stubbornness and dedication to his ideas. As soon as he had jumped ship in San Francisco harbor he had set about devoting his life to the easing of the lot of his fellow men. The course of this easing lay in promoting the widest possible distribution of Patch's Elixir of Life, Good for Man and Beast, a concoction of Old Tamarack whiskey, river water and licorice juice.

16

Through the years, thousands of cowboys, ranchers, homesteaders and miners drank the noxious brew and claimed to benefit. The red-and-gold show wagon which was both abode and place of business to Chief Jim Patch became a familiar visitor to each successive boom town of the west. And the Sweet Singing Princess of The Plains, who began somewhere to ride at his side, made the troupe even more welcome than did the bright-blue bottles.

No child of his generation had traveled more constantly than Adam Patch. He knew the Kansas cow towns, the Montana and Dakota camps. He endured the heat of Tombstone and saw the rapscallion greed of Creed and Central City.

He missed Alaska only because during its heyday he was in Boston fulfilling the grave-side vow made by James Patrick to his Irish God. For despite the old man's boast that he had saved a thousand lives with his elixir, despite his treasured certificates from the diploma mill called the Adirondack College for Teachers and Doctors, Jim had lacked the ability to rally the Princess' failing strength, and Molly had died quietly an hour after Adam's birth.

Standing beside the grave on the windy mountainside with the blanket-wrapped infant cradled in his powerful arms, James Patrick had watched her rude coffin lowered into the bleak Nevada earth, and had sworn his oath that Molly's son would have the finest training to bring the arts of healing to the west.

Adam was thinking of his father and the oath as his long strides took him back into town. The off-shift crowds were as thick as usual, surging through the night in search of entertainment, but it was a sobered crowd. The news of the trouble at Gopher had permeated the town, and men spoke in low tones as if everyone in the distant mountain camp was already marked for death.

In the Northern the games of chance were still idle, and it seemed to Patch that no one had moved since his departure. With easy grace he reached the bar and swung up to its top. Standing there he commanded a view of the whole long room.

Around him the buzz of conversation died quickly, and he looked down on the up-turned faces and saw fear, uncertainty and doubt. Most of these men had braved peril all of their lives, but there was an instinctive fear of sickness, and the word plague held a terror generations old.

He raised his hands and his voice. "I've

just talked to Indian Jake," he said. "The boys at Gopher are in a bad way. First their road washed out in a flash flood. Then they were snowed in, and now they have the fever."

He paused, watching their reactions, then went on. "I'm going up there. I'll take what supplies I can by wagon, as far as I can drive, but from there on I'll need help."

There was a tide of movement in the room as men shifted their positions uneasily, and he saw the withdrawn look come into the faces and knew that each man was remembering the harsh stories they had heard of the mysterious fever.

His chin thrust forward, he waited through the silence that stretched too long. There would be no volunteers, that much was plain. He should have known, he thought, and already his quick mind was searching for some other solution, some way in which to take the needed supplies to the stricken camp.

And then one man moved and stood forward. Adam Patch looked at him in surprise.

Lindsay Stewart was a golden man, shorter than Patch by several inches. His eyes were an odd color, and glowed like those of an aroused cat when he was interested. They were glowing now.

"Count me in, Doctor."

He smiled, pushing ostentatiously through the press of men as if he would draw them into motion by his own surging passage. But the maneuver failed and the ranks closed up behind him to continue staring in dumb refusal.

Patch considered, calculating, remembering the rumors that thrived around Stewart. Scion of five generations of Tidewater aristocrats, the man had grown up in the poverty brought on by the wreckage the carpet-baggers had made of postwar Virginia. He had drifted west to escape the rot of defeat that had engulfed so many of his class.

A gentleman born, his manners entirely out of place on the desert frontier, he had left his mark in Alaska and in Tonopah before coming on south to Goldfield. He was reputed to be one of the best shots in town, one of the best horsemen, and there was little doubt that he was the camp's leading lawyer.

Patch had never known him to volunteer for anything, to take part in any local enterprise or civic endeavor. He held very much to himself out of business hours, was seldom seen in the saloons that served the town as social clubs. He never sat at the card tables. But there were indications that he was not unknown at the better houses where women were the sole attraction.

Patch shrugged now, saying, "It's a rough country we're going into, Counselor."

"I know," said Liindsay Stewart. "I was in Gopher last summer." He smiled, and there was a mocking turn to his delicate lips as if he found it amusing that Patch should question his ability to make the trip. "I think I'll survive."

Patch made his decision, nodding, though there were a dozen men in the big room whom he would rather have had with him to face the rigors that experience told him lay ahead.

He looked directly at the sheriff, Bert Bell, who stood talking to Rickard at the far end of the bar. The blocky man neither looked up nor made any indication that he had heard the appeal. A wave of resentment against these people rode up through Patch and his mouth was hard as he jumped back to the floor.

He would have no trouble getting teamsters and wagons to carry the medicine and supplies across the desert to the foot of the mountains, but once the way turned up toward the higher country, once they had to walk and carry the load, most of the hired men would turn back.

Well, he would have to solve that in its own time. He turned brusquely toward the door, but Rickard called his name and came up.

"You're taking on a load, Doc," the saloon man said. "What did anyone in Gopher ever do for you?"

Patch looked at him steadily. "Nothing."

"A rattail outfit and a ragtail camp. Sam Dohne is the greatest thief unhung. He's so low that even Soapy Smith couldn't stomach him. He ran him out of Alaska."

"I know."

"And the men with him are the scum of the country. Nobody else would work for him. No other kind would follow him."

"I know that too."

"You're very young," said Rickard, "and you're fired up with serving your fellow men. You're a good doctor, Adam, and a cool-headed gambler, but you don't protect yourself in the clinches."

Patch turned away.

Rickard said, "Wait." He swung around, climbing onto a chair pulled from a nearby table, and sent his voice across the room.

"I'm not going up to Gopher," he said. "And I think the Doc is a fool to try, but I admire him for it. He'll need supplies and hands. I'll start it off with five hundred dollars."

He reached out, lifting a hat from the nearest man's head, and held it upside down. The gold coins rang as they tumbled into the deep crown. It passed from hand to hand, then along the bar, and the nest of coins grew as the donors eased their consciences.

At Patch's side Lindsay Stewart's voice held a bite. "That's our Goldfield," he said. "Generous with their wealth, careless with it, you might say. But not one in a hundred will stir out of here to face that fever and cold."

Patch looked at him curiously. "And why are you going?"

The lawyer seemed to ponder his answer. "You might say I'm bored and this offers a change. You might say I know about Sam's ball of gold and am interested in it."

Patch raised his eyebrows. "Where did you hear about that ball?"

Stewart's smile mocked him. "I talked to Indian Jake just after you left the Collins' house."

"I left him asleep."

Stewart nodded. "He heard me talking to Mary and woke up. He may not have any ears, but he hears real sharp."

"How did you happen to be there?"

"I'd heard the news too. I waited outside until you left."

Suspicion touched Patch and he watched the other sharply. "Why did you wait? Why keep out of sight?"

Stewart gave him a tight-lipped smile. "Doctor," he said in his soft voice, "when you know me better you will also know that I have a reason for everything I do."

Patch started to say, "What kind of an answer is that?" Then he checked himself and shrugged. This was his only help at the moment. He would not run it off, but he would watch.

"All right. Mary Collins is going with us."

"She told me."

"It's a hell of a place to take a woman."

Stewart shrugged. "Try to avoid it. What are you going to do for packers?"

"I'm going back and talk to Jake, ask him for the names of a dozen Indians. There are always plenty of braves hanging around the camp, waiting for a bottle of whiskey or a handout."

The lawyer raised an eyebrow. "Can you trust them? They won't like the idea of the fever. . . ."

Patch shrugged. "They'll go if Jake tells

24

them to. He's big medicine where they're concerned."

Lindsay Stewart chuckled. "I know another way to get men, all you need."

"How's that?"

"Spread the word about Sam Dohne's ball of gold. There are enough toughs in Goldfield to pack in everything you'd want for a year, if they saw a chance of getting their hands on that nugget."

Patch's grin was thin. "There are enough toughs in Gopher now. I'd rather have the Indians to handle."

Rickard came up behind them then, carrying the hat. It was now so loaded with coins that he needed both hands to support the bulging crown.

"Here you go, Doc. Conscience money."

Patch nodded. "Give it to Stewart. He's the business manager for this expedition. And you might help him locate three wagons, some horses and supplies. I'll have the medicine at the store."

He turned away, saying nothing more, and left the saloon.

CHAPTER THREE

The Patch Patent Medicine Emporium was the flaming realization of Jim Patch's second dream. His first had been to see his son become a real doctor, and the red-and-yellow show wagon had traveled endless weary miles while he collected enough money for Adam's education. But it was retired now, reposing beneath the blanketing dust in the tight shed behind the store building, and Jim Patch no longer wandered from town to town and camp to camp.

He spent his full time in the raw building, spinning his stories of the wide frontier, still peddling his elixir but now bragging that the cases ranked against the wall behind the long counter contained every remedy known to the United States Patent Office.

The store was big, spacious, gaudy. The pillars separating the four show windows were painted red and gold after the original wagon and Jim Patch was not above digging out the battered banjo to sing for special customers the old songs that had drawn the crowds to him across the land. The aging voice still held a trace of the Irish tenor that had been famous in his youth.

He was sitting on a stool before the money drawer when his son came in. He was a short man, only five feet five against his dark son's six foot one, and he was the picture of sartorial splendor from the top of his beaver plug to the soles of his hand-sewn boots.

He looked up, saying in a waspish voice, "Where have you been? It's an hour since I heard about your damn-fool speech in the Northern."

Adam Patch had long since become accustomed to his father's mercurial moods and paid small attention to the changes. "I've been up at the Collins' house," he said softly, "arranging with Indian Jake for packers."

Jim Patch sniffed. He had from time to time posed as an Indian chief in the pursual of his profession, but he had no use for the real-life red man.

"Scalawag packers for a thankless mission. There are sick people in Goldfield, and they won't cut your throat to get out of paying your fee."

"And there are doctors here to look after them."

The older Patch glowered. "You could catch the fever yourself. That would be the end of you, and for what?" He found a cigar in the pocket of his embroidered vest, bit off the end angrily and lit it with care, speaking off-handedly between the studied puffs, "I sent for Clara."

Adam had started toward the rear of the store where a connecting door led to his consulting room. He stopped, turning.

27

"Why did you do that?"

"So she could talk some sense into your thick Irish skull. A woman should have some say when the man she's marked to marry aims to prance into a rattlesnake den."

Adam Patch started to argue, then smiled to himself, recognizing the jealous concern beneath his father's disgruntlement. He shrugged and went on into his office. With the certainness of practice he moved to the small storeroom at the side and began setting out the drugs and equipment he wanted with him. He had almost finished when the sound of the office door being opened made him turn.

Clara Holister stood hesitantly on the threshold, her soft brown eyes wide on him, the black hair of her French mother coiffed in the high, shining pile with which she tried to add to her diminutive stature.

She came slowly in, her gaze questioning, trying to gauge his mood, and her voice was small with the child-like quality that he always had found intriguing.

"Your father says you are going to Gopher."

He nodded, turning back to his medicines.

"Why?" A trace of petulance rose in her tone, as if she were displeased at his not answering.

He put down the package he held and came out of the storeroom, taking her small shoulders in his hands and smiling down at her. His voice was gentle but firm, and there was that in it which brooked no argument.

"I am a doctor, Clara. You know that."

She pulled away from him and her cheeks flushed to a dark tone. "So you're a doctor and there is sickness in Gopher. I know what you're going to say, it's your duty to go, but. . . ."

He turned away and went back to his packing. She caught her breath and followed him angrily.

"Adam Patch. Don't you ever dare to walk away from me."

He swung back swiftly, pantherlike, and she saw the gaunt tightness in his face.

"Clara." He was still speaking with a certain amount of control. "My father had no right to send for you."

"You would have left town without telling me?"

"I make calls on the sick every day without telling you."

She tossed her head. "That's different. Those people are in Goldfield, and they haven't got the fever. My uncle died of the fever in Tonopah. Did you know that?"

He forced himself to patience. At times she acted as if she were a little child, and he had found it amusing. But when she began to interfere in his work it became something which must be settled between them.

"I understand how you feel, my dear, but if you are going to be a doctor's wife, you must realize that the needs of the patient come first. Every doctor learns it. Every doctor's wife must learn it too."

Her eyes widened on him. "You actually mean that you would think of them before you would think of me?"

He hunted for words to make her understand. "It's a question of the degree of need," he said. "If you needed me as much as a patient did, naturally I'd think of you first. But I accept a responsibility when I take on a patient, because he is trusting me with his most precious possession — his life."

Her face had a strained look. "Yes, of course, but. . . ."

"There isn't any but." He tried to speak gently. "You have to let me be the judge of whether your need is greater than my patient's, or merely a whim."

"A whim. . . ." The words came out of her in a startled gasp and he realized that he had never before seen her thoroughly angry.

She stared at him, her eyes black as jet, then she spun on her heel and marched out of the office.

He almost went after her, then shook his head and turned to finish the task of packing. This was not the time to pursue the argument, he thought. Better to allow her to cool off, then discuss the problem with her objectively.

The outer door opened again and for a moment he thought it was Clara returning; then his father's short form appeared and Adam Patch frowned. The last person he wanted to talk to at this time was his father.

Jim Patch ambled self-consciously over to lean against a corner of the table, the cigar clenched in the corner of his rosebud mouth, his face distorted into a half scowl.

"Have a fight?"

"That," said Adam Patch, closing the last box, "is really none of your business."

"No," his father admitted, "it isn't, strictly speaking. But you're still pretty young."

"That I'll grow out of if I live long enough."

"Keeping you alive long enough is my present concern. That was my idea in sending for Clara. She's still pretty young too. May I tell you something about women?"

"No, thank you."

"Women," said Jim Patch as if Adam had not spoken, "need to feel important."

"For God's sake," said Adam Patch, "don't lecture me on elemental psychology. Everybody has to feel important."

"And Clara's a little spoiled." Jim Patch had the ability to follow his own chain of thought without being distracted. "She's used to having her own way. I grant you she needs a bit of settling, but don't push it too fast. Her father owns a lot of stock in some of Goldfield's principal mines. It's a good match for you."

"You're a snob," said the younger man. "I'm not marrying her for her money. I don't need it. I can make my own money."

"It isn't for money," said his father. "You are a good doctor, Adam. You could be a great one. But to really be somebody a man must have a wife who can keep pace with him. Don't throw it away, son. Clara has been broadminded. She doesn't like your gambling, but she hasn't so much as mentioned it."

"Not yet," said Adam, "but she will. When the wagons come, have that stuff loaded on them." He indicated the cases he had packed. "I'm going to change clothes."

Without waiting for his father's answer he turned and left the store. Outside there was

32

a stairway at the north end of the building and he mounted to the second floor, where he maintained his living quarters.

He changed rapidly, trading the tailored town clothes for rough wool pants, a heavy shirt and a sheeplined coat. From the bottom drawer he drew the belt and gun, which he seldom wore in town, and fastened it in place around the flatness of his hips.

Then he came again downstairs, and by this time Lindsay Stewart was waiting for him before the show windows. The lawyer also had changed to rough clothing, and somehow it made him look smaller, more delicate than usual.

In answer to Patch's questioning glance he said, "The wagons will be loading in a few minutes. I got horses for the packers and for us. Come along, we have about half an hour to eat."

He turned without Patch's assent and led the way across the width of the dusty street, ducking gracefully between the freight wagons that kept up an endless chain of movement twenty-four hours each day.

Goldfield never slept. The mines worked two twelve-hour shifts each day. The saloons, the principal business houses, even the hundred-odd assay offices whose main service was buying stolen ore, all kept their doors open around the clock.

There had never been a camp like this in history, for here the gold was free-milling ore, at times running forty dollars to the pound. An average miner could steal two hundred dollars' worth each shift and spend it in a single night.

There were still people on the street, although the clock was nearing four, but the life was gone and they moved quietly.

"The hour of truth," said Lindsay Stewart at Patch's side. "The hour of truce, when man's vitality is at its lowest ebb."

Patch looked at him and Stewart smiled faintly. "This is the time for self-re-examination, when our past sins rise up like specters in the fading night and twist our souls with bitterness. All anyone wants at this moment is to be left alone to nurse his self-condemnation, to sit in judgment on himself and leave others to do the same."

"You sound unhappy."

The lawyer shrugged. "Not unhappy, but life is a stage, people the players for me to watch. Most of the time they are on parade, but at this hour they respect one another's privacy. It's my chance to look at them as they really are."

He led the way into the Elite Restaurant and took a place at one of the scrubbed wooden-topped tables. Patch settled across from him and they gave their order. Then Stewart looked around the room.

"You know most of the people in here, Adam. Ordinarily they'd speak to you."

Patch said nothing, listening, learning more about this slender blond young man than he had guessed before.

Stewart's smile was thin. "I make my point. See Annie Mulrany over at the far table. Two hours ago she stopped me on the street."

Patch glanced toward her. The woman was nearly thirty, usually alert, smiling at any man she met. Now her finery of the evening was wilted, her dyed blond hair falling from place, the sagging lines in the melted make-up telling of worldly disillusionment.

Beyond her sat two gambling dealers from one of the lesser saloons, slumped over their coffee, their hands folded prayerfully around the steaming mugs. There were petty criminals present, the flotsam, the weary. There were three deputies from the sheriff's office, but they were not on duty and did not care. It was a cross section of Goldfield, the richest town in the world.

They ate without further talk, then went back down the street toward the livery. The three freight wagons were drawn up outside the big barn and men with lanterns were securing the loads under the watchful eye of Pop Gilbert, the barn boss.

Pop was a little man with a thin chin whisker that made him look like a bantam goat, and a shock of white hair standing in a brush on his small head. He turned as Patch and Lindsay Stewart came up, his old eyes as bright as if he were still in his twenties instead of crowding eighty.

"Need another hand, Doc?"

Patch grinned at him. "Who'd take care of Goldfield if you came with us?"

Pop spat. "Hell with it. Let the thieving camp look after itself. I'm going along. . . ." He started back into the barn and Patch followed him while Lindsay Stewart remained outside to supervise the rest of the loading.

"Look, Pop —" Patch had no desire to hurt the old man's feelings, but he had enough on his hands without being saddled by a man who might die of exposure. "Tell you what you do. You stay here. I'm probably going to need more supplies than we have. If I do, I'll send back one of the Indians and you take care of getting stuff together for me. Right?"

"You think I haven't got the strength." Pop's voice was accusing. "Let me tell you something, Adam Patch. I can outride and outwalk three quarters of the men in this country. I'm going, and you ain't stopping me."

Adam sighed. He already had a woman to worry about. It seemed now that there was no escape from taking Pop. He turned back into the runway, and stopped.

Bryant Holister had come into the barn from the rear, walking across the hay-strewn floor with a certain confidence that told of drunken purpose.

Adam Patch watched him in silence. Holister was big, standing a good six foot three, heavy shouldered, with big arms that would have done more service to a blacksmith than to one of the town's leading stockbrokers. He came to an abrupt stop in front of Patch, staring from eyes not quite in focus.

"So. Here you are."

Patch did not answer. He had small love for this hulking brother of the girl he was expecting to marry. Holister had already added considerably to the family fortune. He had promoted a dozen mines along the Goldfield reef and half a hundred among the smaller towns that had sprung up like satellites around the larger camp.

Most of his promotions had been sold through the East, for he was reputed to have a longer sucker list than any of the other two hundred brokers gracing the local stock exchange. Also, it was general knowledge that he was not too careful in the properties of which he sold shares to the distant, gullible investors. Few of the mines he had helped to finance had ever produced much shippable ore.

"Clara says you're going to Gopher."

Patch merely nodded.

"You're an ass," said Bryant Holister. "You always were, and I for one say good riddance. I tried to warn Clara that you're no better than a shady gambler, that the only reason you want to marry her is for our money."

"Your opinion." Adam Patch spoke without expression, then turned again for the front of the barn.

Bryant Holister thrust out a hamlike hand and caught his shoulder, spinning him around.

"Now you listen to me. . . ."

"Take your hand off me."

Holister laughed nastily. Instead of releasing his grip he tightened his fingers.

"I'll let you go when I've had my say. My sister came home back apiece, crying her eyes out. I don't know what you said to her, but I'm going to make you eat the words, whatever they were." He used his free hand to swing a clubbing blow at Patch's head.

Adam wrenched loose and jumped back, almost surprised. "You're drunk."

"I'm not so drunk I can't take care of you. When I finish you'll need all the medicine that quack father of yours keeps in that fancy store."

He charged. Patch side-stepped and then, on balance, swung a curving hook at the man's face. The blow stopped Holister for a full moment, partly sobering him. He shook his head, trying to clear it, then with a great roar he dived in, trying to wrap his big arms around Patch's slighter body.

Again Patch side-stepped, and used his fist against Holister's cheek, feeling the shock of the impact run back through his arm, wondering if he had split a knuckle.

But he had small time to wonder, for although the bigger man was shaken he did not go down. His hands found Patch and dragged him into a bearlike grip that closed relentlessly in a compressing vice. They dropped to the floor together.

Patch had a confused look at Pop Gilbert's hopping form. The old man had run out of the office, seized a hay fork and was circling them, dancing, holding the fork

39

raised as if he sought to stab Holister in the back.

Patch yelled at him, not so much in concern for the other man as in the fear that, as they rolled, the old barn man might sink the fork into his own body by mistake.

The yell surprised Holister and he loosened his embrace for a fraction of time, and Patch used the moment to break from it, to roll and come up to his knees.

Holister lay where he was, glaring upward. Patch wiped his mouth with the back of his hand and tasted blood from a cut inside his cheek where he had bumped it on his attacker's head. Then he spat and rose, not quite steady on his feet.

Holister followed him up, eying him with a new respect. Patch moved in swiftly and as the man retreated he chopped with both hands, short, hard blows to the ribs, and finally as Holister's arms came down he caught him squarely on the chin.

Holister fell. He was not out but he made no effort to rise, and Patch turned away to find that Lindsay Stewart and the teamsters made a grouped audience in the wide doorway.

The lawyer gave him a small, one-sided grin. "Operation performed with dispatch," he said, "but there are two people who won't forget this night's work soon. The course of true love seldom runs smoothly, friend Adam."

Patch wiped his mouth again, leaving a smear of blood across one cheek. Suddenly he realized that he did not care. The thought surprised him for Clara Holister was a very attractive woman.

Chapter Four

They went out of town almost unnoticed, a slow moving line. Lindsay Stewart and Mary Collins rode in the lead, the three wagons following and Patch, Indian Jake with his packers and Pop Gilbert at the rear.

The old liveryman had appeared already mounted, a rifle in the boot under his wiry leg, and Patch had known no way to discourage his coming.

They followed the main road north toward Tonopah. Even at this early hour, in the wide desert reaches it was one of the most highly traveled highways in Nevada. An endless skein of freight wagons crawled tongue to tail-gate twenty-four hours each day; the northbound carrying ore for the mills at the older camp, those going south piled high with food and furniture, mining machinery and all the stuff needed by the isolated camp.

They were five miles out of town before they turned into the side road which angled northwest, toward the snow-covered peaks of the distant mountains.

As soon as they lost sight of the main trail they were alone in some of the most desolate country in the world. Flinty, sandy soil, crisscrossed by volcanic upthrusts of rock, stretched in all directions, laced by old arroyos and gullies left by forgotten flash floods.

Dawn came slowly, the graying light making the land seem more sinister than it actually was, and Mary Collins shivered as her horse picked its way among the old ruts of the track.

"Cold?" Lindsay Stewart looked at her in concern.

She shook her head. "Not really. It's simply that I never seem to get used to this land, to its bleakness, its ugliness."

He nodded. "So ugly that it's beautiful. So dangerous that it's enchanting."

She looked at him. "If it's so dangerous I wonder that you chose to come with us."

He met her eyes directly. "You don't need to wonder."

Color climbed in her cheeks that were

already flushed by the chill wind.

"Please, I thought we had agreed not to mention that again. I'm married. I don't need to remind you, do I?"

Stewart made an impatient gesture with his gloved hand. "To an oaf. To a fool who lets Sam Dohne twist him around his crooked finger for his own purposes. You can't look at me fully and tell me you love him, that you have ever truly loved Clint Collins."

Her head lifted. "Not love him, perhaps." She said it slowly as if searching her mind for the proper words. "But I am grateful. Perhaps that is as near to love as I will ever know, Mr. Stewart."

"You called me Lindsay once."

"Before you made me self-conscious with your attentions. Please. I wish you had not come."

"Because you're afraid that if you're with me constantly you'll finally have to admit that I'm the man for you."

"It isn't that. I admire you for what you've done. I was very thankful when you helped Clint through his trouble."

A savage note crept into Stewart's tone. "I should have let him go to prison and rot there. I would have, except for you."

"And now you want payment?"

The Southern man winced. "What kind do you take me for? Have I ever given any indication that I expected anything improper from you? Don't be unfair. I want to marry you, can't you understand that? I've known many women in my life, and apparently few of them have found me unattractive, but I have never really wanted anyone but you. If you'll accept me, we'll get out of this country. We'll go anywhere you name, do anything you want to do."

"I am married."

"Words, phrases. I can get you a divorce."

"I don't believe in divorce, Mr. Stewart."

He looked at her helplessly. Through his whole life Lindsay Stewart had usually managed to talk anyone into any act he desired them to make; yet this girl defeated him. There was a finality in her that turned argument aside before it was wholly formulated. He shook his head sadly.

"I expected better of you. I really did."

"There are several things you do not understand," she said, and both her eyes and her tone had grown more gentle. "I was raised in an orphanage. When I was sixteen I ran away to escape being sent out as a servant girl as my friends had been. I met an actor and married him, not because I loved him but because I didn't know what

44

else to do."

She was silent, remembering. When she went on her voice had changed. "He died, in a little Montana mining town. The show moved on and I was stranded. I didn't know how to do anything except housework, and there was no one there who wanted to hire that done. The only other way I could make a living was in a fancy house. You see, the townspeople had marked me as part of the show troupe and in their eyes there was no difference."

Lindsay Stewart flinched again, this time for a different reason.

"That was where Clint Collins showed up. I was being put out of the boarding house. He was staying there. He took me away with him. I thought I knew what he intended, but I was too tired, too despondent to care what happened. Instead, he married me.

"I don't care what he is or what he's done. He helped me when I needed help and I won't walk out on him. I couldn't live with myself if I did."

Stewart nodded reluctantly. "You couldn't, being you. Mary, I've known few women with your loyalty. I think that's what first attracted me. Most of the women I've known were innately selfish. I'm sorry I spoke. But just remember, I pay you the

45

highest compliment it is mine to give. I love you." He wheeled his horse suddenly and doubled back along the train at a half run, pulling up beside Adam.

"You've eaten dust for a while, Doctor, let me take my turn."

Patch looked at him in surprise, noting the unusual strain in the man's face, the brusqueness of his manner. Then he nodded, rode around the slow, creaking wagons and reined in to ride beside the girl.

She gave him a small smile which he thought was forced, then looked off again at the distant snow-capped mountains.

"How long before we get to the canyon?"

"Sometime tomorrow."

Her face tightened. "This fever, what chance does a man have if he catches it?"

Patch shrugged, wanting her to have no illusions. "That I can't answer since I don't know what it actually is."

"But you must have some idea. I thought doctors knew all about such things."

His mouth turned down with an old frustration. "There are a great many things doctors do not know. Far too many. This fever I suspect is a virulent form of grippe, but I can't be sure. About the only cure we know for such things is warmth, rest, good care. They're not easy to find in a town like

Gopher."

She looked at him levelly. "I'm a fair nurse. My first husband died of consumption. I took care of him for months."

He was startled. He had not known that she had been married before. To him she seemed almost too young, and he found that he watched her with an awakening curiosity. She had poise beyond her years and her speech was good, without the grammatical faults so common on the frontier.

But how did such a woman happen to be married to Clint Collins? Clint was a big man, easygoing, with a bent for practical humor that made him popular with most men. Yet he was weak and vacillating, and he had gotten himself into serious trouble by unloading a salted mine on some Eastern investors. It was common talk in Goldfield that Clint would have gone to prison had it not been for Lindsay Stewart's shrewdness.

Patch rode silently, speculating over the air of tension between the lawyer and this girl. He was not inclined by nature to pay much attention to other people's affairs, nor did it bother him that Stewart might be dallying with a married woman. The lawyer's reputation was such that this would be no surprise.

But he felt a disappointment about Mary

Collins. Without really thinking about it, he had expected a higher character in her. She did not interrupt his thoughts. They rode until noon and then stopped in a sheltered draw.

The Indians squatted beyond the cooking fire in a silent semicircle. Mary Collins watched them disinterestedly, thinking how great a change a few short years had wrought. She was used to them now, used to seeing them around the town cadging food, running errands, performing the most menial work while most of their small earnings went for liquor.

Patch brought her a plate and she ate with relish, aware suddenly that she had had nothing since the night before. Clint would be glad to see her and the thought was warming, but it also caused her to look toward Stewart and her face took on a thoughtful expression.

Life with the lawyer would be far different than the life she had with Collins. It would be far different than any life she had yet lived. The thought was exciting however much she tried to put it down, for Stewart had breeding, education and an intellect that she had never met with before.

And then her gaze turned to Patch who stood quietly beside the fire. His face was almost as dark as those of the Indians, almost as impassive. She forced her mind away from Stewart, trying to guess what the doctor was thinking about. Was it the sick in Gopher? The hard trail ahead? A woman? She would have been amazed and somewhat upset to know that his thoughts were directed on herself.

The night camp was under the shadow of a bleak butte that reared out of the scarred desert. The mountains seemed incredibly nearer in the gathering darkness. The wagons had been pulled together as a windbreak, but the sharp air came through with chilling force, sweeping down in the night draft from the snow above.

Quietly, Lindsay Stewart carried her blankets from the wagon and arranged them in the lea of a small boulder, giving her a trace of privacy from the rest of the camp. He brushed away the loose rocks, leveled the space as much as he could, then dug a hip hole deeper than necessary and partially refilled it with loosened sand.

When he straightened, she thanked him with a small smile, curling herself in the blankets as he left. She lay staring wide-eyed at the awesome arch of the night sky, at the undulating light of the cloud of stars.

The fire died down slowly. The teamsters

and Indians slept beside the wagons. Stewart was a small dark shape across the glowing embers. Adam Patch continued long to sit hunched with his blanket coat backed to the blast of the wind. Pop Gilbert huddled close to him, his old body shielded by a close-held blanket, talking in low tones with Indian Jake, recalling things that had happened long ago; two old men finding companionship in common years.

And at last she slept.

When she roused, the smell of the brush fire was already in the gray morning air. The wind was gone, but replaced by a steady cold that ate through her gathered blankets.

She stirred and Stewart saw her, and came at once with a pail half full of water, warm from the fire. She had never welcomed anything quite so gratefully. Her skin, dried by the wind and dusted with sand, had the gritty feel of coarse sandpaper.

She bent behind her boulder, feeling exposed before all those men even though she was fully dressed, and washed her face and hands and her rounded arms carefully. Then she rose, emptied the bucket and moved in to the fire.

Without speaking Patch handed her a plate of thick bacon and beans, a cup of smoking coffee. The black liquid seared her lips and the rim of the metal cup bit at them, but she drank, and felt the warmth lift the chill from her blood.

But the morning was still cold when Pop Gilbert led her saddled horse forward and she felt stiff as she mounted.

The tattered ground grew rougher and began to rise. By ten, they were in the foothills and the character of the land changed abruptly. Here water seeped down from the snowbanks and the straggly, sparse growth gave way to stunted trees.

They reached the mouth of the canyon at three, and the wagons could go no further. Indian Jake had not lied. The road ended abruptly where the raging waters had torn it away, the flash flood had come down the chute of the canyon and spread over the flatland, leaving in its wake a scattered profusion of boulders, some as large as a small house.

It took time then to rig the pack saddles, to transfer the goods and medicines from the wagons to the horses. From the brittleness of the morning, the air had turned to desert heat, and the girl sought the shade of mesquite while the men labored antlike in the sun. Stewart urged her not to surrender her horse to the packers, but she shook her head, pointing out that she had promised to be no trouble if Patch allowed her to come along, saying that the beast was needed to carry the supplies.

Patch made no comment. He saw the horses loaded. He instructed the teamsters to wait there until the Indians returned down the mountain. Then he motioned Indian Jake to lead off, and the train again formed and lurched into motion.

They wound upward, the horses turning and twisting to avoid the deep cuts and the huge rocks left by the washout, and Patch was deeply grateful that the spring was still young, that the rains had not started; they would make this canyon too dangerous a track to follow.

Darkness caught them still below the snow and all night they shivered in the roaring downdraft which beat upon them with unrelenting intensity. There was very little shelter from it, but Stewart broke branches from the fragrant junipers and made a bed for Mary Collins in the lea of two boulders.

Adam Patch observed the constant small attentions with which the lawyer tried to protect the girl. Stewart interested him. The man was so highly polished, yet showed no warmth within. He was like jade, warm on the surface only. Patch guessed that Stewart would obey all of the rules of conduct laid down for the guidance of a gentleman as long as they served his purpose, and no longer. There seemed a streak of ruthlessness in the smaller man that had taken him to the top and would keep him there.

He was not avaricious, Patch felt. He showed the contempt for money held by so many who had made theirs, made it easily and knew that they could always make more.

It was the uncertain people of the world who knew avarice, who held grimly to what they had, always fearful that if it slipped through their fingers they would never be able to recover what they had lost.

Yet with the girl, Stewart was gentleness itself. It was as if he had opened wide his shielding armor.

They were moving again before daylight, walking through the dawn cold. They reached the snow at ten in the morning and here unpacked the horses and strapped on snowshoes. The horses were left in the care of three Indians. The packers hefted the burdens to their shoulders and the expedition started up the tortuous trail behind old Jake.

It took them the better part of two days to reach the stricken camp.

CHAPTER FIVE

Gopher did not know whether it was in California or Nevada. It sat in a canyon near the crest of the high mountains which served as the dividing line between the two states. No one cared, since there had never been much law in the sprawling camp.

The original strike had been made three years before by two cowboys turned prospectors who, after doing a minimum of development work, sold the property to Sam Dohne and Clint Collins.

Working under the name of the Gopher Mining Company they had driven a haulage tunnel into the bleak canyon side, nearly three-quarters of a mile. The camp had boomed, other prospects had been developed until the town boasted some twelve hundred inhabitants.

But there were less than a hundred left when Indian Jake, looking like a gaunt scarecrow in his blanket coat, led the long line of packers up the last rise of the snow-choked canyon and into the single straggling main street.

The canyon was so narrow that the backs of the log buildings which flanked the thoroughfare were tight against the rising rock walls, and the board sidewalk at the street's edge was barely wide enough for two people to pass without bumping shoulders.

Adam Patch, following the extreme end of the line of weary marchers, could not help contrasting this scene of desolation with the gay bustle of Goldfield. For all its geographical isolation, Goldfield was a modern town, rich, tolerant and carefree, a young and healthy town that took nothing seriously including the river of wealth flowing from its mines.

Coming into Gopher was like coming into a place accursed. Those few people on the street were gaunt and empty-eyed. There was no laughter here, nor even any greeting. They watched with no show of interest as the line of Indian packers approached the store building. Fear and hunger had squeezed all but breath out of them.

The company store building was the largest structure in the quarter mile of the single street. It perched in a place where the canyon wall receded perhaps twenty feet and so was much deeper than its flanking neighbors.

It sat back from the narrow sidewalk, allowing a six-foot-wide porch, and on the porch, between the two center doors, squatted the ball of gold.

Fully two feet in diameter, the ball glittered dully in the late-afternoon sunlight, mocking those around it for their inability to carry it away. Half a million dollars' worth of the precious metal. Men had murdered for far less, yet what good was it to anyone standing there? It could not check the fever, could not produce a single sack of flour. Gopher had gold aplenty, but it had not purchased relief for its people.

The packers stopped in a double line, standing patient as mules and showing no more interest in their surroundings than the citizenry showed in them. Gradually, people began shifting toward the porch, unconsciously drawn by the activity there, but no one yet bothered to question or comment on the newcomers.

And then Sam Dohne appeared in the store doorway and brought animation to the sluggish scene. Sam was nearing sixty. His head was round and his girth too thick for his height. In a country which had attracted thieves and con men in droves, Sam stood out as their natural leader.

Story had it that he had escaped hanging in Dodge only because the rope had broken, that he had been run out of Alaska by Soapy Smith, king of the con men, and had hurriedly left camp after camp until at last he

56

had landed in Gopher. He came bouncing forward now, rubbing his plump hands together and grinning broadly.

"Hi, Doc. Welcome. Welcome indeed. Thanks for coming for me."

Adam Patch did not like Sam Dohne and made no effort at pretense. "We didn't come for you, Sam, and I'll see that you don't make a profit from these supplies."

Sam Dohne never allowed himself to be insulted. His grin widened. "Sure," he said. "I'm with you, Doc." Then he walked on to where Mary Collins had sunk down on the edge of the porch. "Your man's up at the mine, Mary. He'll be down pretty soon."

"Then he's all right?" Relief made her voice sing.

"All right? Sure." Sam Dohne laughed. "You thought maybe he had the fever, eh? The fever ain't been invented that can touch a couple of burglars like Clint and me." He raised his voice to call loudly, and an aproned clerk came out of the store on the run.

"Show these war whoops where to stow the grub. Doc, where you want to set up shop? We got the sick ones camped over in the lodge hall now."

"As good a place as any," Patch said. He motioned to his train and they followed

Dohne up the twisting street to where the hall sat, well separated from any other building.

It was a twenty-by-thirty structure, backed snugly against the canyon wall which had been dug out to allow for the dimensions. At the far end was a small raised platform, both a podium for speakers and a bandstand at dance time.

But now, twenty beds had been set up in the dim interior, and even with the little light Patch could see that most of them were in use. The windows were all shuttered, keeping the foul air inside, and Patch turned to Pop Gilbert.

"Get those shutters open. I want as much air in here as possible."

Sam Dohne objected. "Night air's bad for the fever, Doc. Everybody knows that."

Without looking at him Patch said, "If you're a doctor why did you send Jake for me?"

"No offense. No offense." Dohne took a half step backward as if he feared that Patch might hit him. "It's only that some of the boys ain't going to like the idea."

"I'm not worried about those who are well enough to object." Patch studied the room. It was overly warm and held the dirty smell common to buildings that have not been properly aired, but beyond this there hung the cloying, sweetish odor of sickness. He spoke to Pop Gilbert again.

"Next, bring a couple of buckets of water and put them on the stove." He nodded toward the potbellied wood stove in the middle of the room, its heat spreading out to temper the chill mountain wind.

Gilbert bobbed his head and ducked back through the door. Patch called in the Indians who carried his medicines, directing them to put the cases on the table on the podium. Then he and Dohne trailed them out and back to the store. Others of the packers waited there, and as he approached, Patch saw two of them on the porch, their shoulders against the ball of gold. They pushed at it and it began to move, sluggishly roiling toward the edge of the porch. Behind him Sam Dohne swore in Piute.

"Get your greasy fingers off of that."

The Indians jumped away and Patch grunted. "You don't actually think they could get it down the canyon?"

Sam Dohne laughed, a rasping sound. "There's plenty in camp would like to try. I'll give any two men half of it if they can lift that ball."

Patch had little interest in the gold ball. He called to Indian Jake where the squaw man sat against a porch post, apparently near exhaustion. The old man looked up slowly, his leathered face and stringy hair making him seem more native than most of the packers.

"Tell your boys to go and camp above town. The less they're around this place the better I'll like it. I don't want them getting the fever, and especially I don't want them taking it back to Goldfield." He pulled a handful of gold coins from his pocket and counted them out. "One for each."

Jake shook his greasy head. "Too much, Doc."

"Give it to them."

"Waste. They'd just get drunk."

"It's their privilege. The poor devils, they don't get much out of life. Tell them to start back in the morning, and to leave the horses with someone to guard them down at the bottom. We'll need them when we start back."

He looked around then, asking the clerk, "Where's Mrs. Collins?"

"The lawyer fellow took her over to the hotel."

Patch nodded. "Got any mops in the store?"

"Sure."

"Send four over to the lodge hall, and four

men to swing them."

He turned away then, retracing his steps to the room of sick men. In the light from the now-opened windows he approached the first bed, seeing at once that the man lying there was dead.

Dohne had followed him silently as far as the doorway, and saw from Patch's face what had happened. He swore.

"Joe Moon. Yesterday noon he was walking around as healthy as you and me. About seven o'clock they found him down, in the street, and lugged him in here."

Patch bent above the dead man. The lips were very red, but beginning to blacken. The cheeks were already turning dark. He looked as if he had choked to death.

"Like his heart blew up and stuck in his throat," Dohne said. He had moved to the doctor's side, and there was more feeling in his heavy voice than Patch had ever heard there.

Sam Dohne was as cold-blooded as they came, but even Sam was moved by this silent terror that struck down apparently healthy men in the street, killed them in a matter of hours.

Patch looked at the man. He did not appear afraid, but awe struck rather. Patch wondered if Dohne, knowing the danger of infection here, was too stupid to fear or had an unsuspected courage.

He said, "Have you got a couple of men who will touch the body, will move it?"

Dohne nodded solemnly. "Harry Janas and Kid Beale. They both got it early. They beat it. They figure they can't get it again."

Patch was surprised. Kid Beale had escaped the Goldfield jail seven months before, having been held there on a murder charge, suspected of slaying an assayer. He was a small man, not young, with a record of violence that ran back to the Kansas frontier. He was reported to have killed six men, yet here he was in Gopher, offering himself to carry out the victims of the fever.

Dohne saw the doctor's look and guessed his thought. His round mouth moved in a twisting smile.

"Nobody's all one way, Doc, good or bad."

It was a truth that Patch was well aware of, but hearing it voiced by Dohne was another surprise. But there was little time to think of these things at the moment.

"What have you been doing about burials?" he asked.

Sam Dohne shrugged. "Not much we can do, Doc. The canyon floor is rock, with not more than two, three inches of dirt over it. But there's an old prospect hole maybe fifty-

or seventy-five-feet deep. We been dumping them down there and throwing some rocks over them. It's the best we had."

Patch nodded. "Good. When they put this one down, spread some kerosene and light it."

Dohne's expression turned to horror, and Patch added, "We've got to clean the camp, Sam, to kill the source of the disease. Now, are there plenty of blankets and mattresses in town?"

Dohne drew a deep breath. "Hell, yes. We've only got a twelfth of the people we had a month ago."

Patch pointed to the bed, talking rapidly, keeping his voice businesslike. There were many ugly things necessary to be done and there was no time to argue with Sam Dohne.

"I want the blankets and mattress burned too. I want the bed washed down with hot water and strong lye soap, and then if you've got enough whiskey, wash it with that."

Sam stared at him, then began an almost hysterical laugh. "Doc, I've heard of whiskey being used for lots of things, but never to wash a bed in. Yeah, we got plenty. We laid in a supply to last the full winter. There's still a hundred kegs back in the storehouse." He turned out of the building, shaking his head.

Patch moved on to the next bed. The man there had apparently been delirious. His legs and arms were tied to the bedposts and a rope circled his middle, pinioning him down. But he was no longer in a delirium. He had sunk into a coma, and although there was still a faint pulse and a flutter of heartbeat, Patch wondered if he would last until the volunteers had carried out the other victim.

Noise at the door made him turn, and he started. Mary Collins was poised on the threshold and even as he watched, she started to come in.

"Keep out of here." His voice was sharper than he intended. "I've enough on my hands without you getting sick."

She had stopped at his peremptory tone. Now she came on, saying in her deep-throated voice, "I came to help."

"You can help most by keeping as far from the fever as you can."

"I told you I know something about nursing." She looked around the bare room, its only color the strip of faded bunting, red and white and blue, draped above the bandstand. Her nose wrinkled in distaste. "This place is worse than a pigpen. I'll need hot water, lots of it."

He didn't argue. He needed help if he was

to help these stricken people. He shrugged, pointing to the two buckets beginning to steam on the stove.

Mary Collins laughed. "My dear man. That wouldn't begin to clean one corner of the room. These men all need to be bathed, and those well enough should be shaved. My husband, even when he was dying, wanted to be shaved every morning. It took me awhile to learn to do it properly."

"You shaved him?"

She said tartly, "I am not entirely helpless just because I am a woman."

Already she was pulling the sweater over her head, rolling up the sleeves of her gray wool dress. She crossed to test the temperature of the water and spoke across her shoulder.

"Send someone to the store for all the rags they have."

"I've got four men coming in with mops. I wish you wouldn't expose yourself here. . . ."

"Why, are you more protected than I am?"

"Well, I'm a doctor. . . ."

"Stuff and nonsense."

Suddenly, unaccountably, he grinned. He swung, striding out of the hall into the biting cold of the early darkness that was creeping down the canyon sides, and headed for the store.

Halfway there he saw Lindsay Stewart emerge from the log hotel and heard him say:

"I put your gear in Room Ten."

"Thanks," said Patch.

Stewart fell into step beside him, his shorter legs somehow managing to match the doctor's long swinging walk.

"Have you seen Mary Collins?"

"She's at the lodge hall."

Quick worry furrowed Stewart's forehead. "She shouldn't be in that poisoned place."

"She shouldn't have left Goldfield. I couldn't stop her and I can't make her leave the hall. Maybe when Collins comes down from the mine she'll listen to him."

He jumped the step to the store porch and continued on inside. A dozen men sat silent and slumped in the jumble of merchandise that crowded the shelves and low counter and cluttered the floor. No one spoke but their eyes watched him.

He ordered the clerk to produce all the hot water possible. He moved quickly, collecting soap, a bolt of cloth to tear into rags, a bucket of whiskey from the keg standing on the rear of the counter.

The eyes followed his every turn, like those of cornered animals, mute with fear of the unknown. A sudden sense of deep responsibility welled within him. He had known it before but never to this extent and he faced away from them that they should not read it in his expression. When he could control it he called again to the clerk.

"As soon as the crew comes down from the mine I want everyone in camp to meet me here. I want to talk to them all together. There'll have to be rules observed if we're to lick this thing. Send someone to the hall for me when they're gathered."

He turned hastily back into the night.

CHAPTER SIX

Adam Patch was amazed at the miracle Mary Collins wrought in the lodge hall within the next hour.

Men arrived with hot water, with mops and brooms and fresh blankets. They came hesitant, uncertain, unwilling to enter the room which housed the sickness, but the example of the girl gave them courage. She moved quickly from one bed to another, bathing the heated bodies, shaving the whiskers from the hollow cheeks, murmuring encouragement to each, and the dull eyes followed her around as if she were some mysterious vision.

Patch stood at the table measuring out medicines and handing them to Lindsay Stewart. The lawyer, after a futile try at making the girl give up the dangerous labor, himself turned in, silently, efficiently helping at whatever appeared to need doing. Between them, he and Patch soon had each of the victims dosed.

Two others died, dropping soundlessly from the living ranks. Kid Beale and his partner brought their two-wheeled cart and made the dark passage to the mine sump.

Three new cases were admitted, cleansed and put to bed on fresh mattresses beneath clean blankets. One of those who was mopping the floor, collapsed. The fear came closer. The cleaning crew stopped to watch Patch care for their fellow, to glance longingly toward the door. Then they looked at the girl and stayed.

Patch was astonished at the way they worked. He recognized several as men wanted in Goldfield for various crimes; hard men, selfish and lawless, yet here they closed ranks and worked ungrudging behind the girl.

For herself, her smile and her manner of hope seemed to do more for the patients than the doctor's medicines.

And then Clint Collins burst in. Patch

turned to see him nearly filling the doorway. He had forgotten how big Collins was. The miner stood there, his blond, curly head bare, the ringlets touched with snow, for it had started to storm half an hour before. Then he came on, striding forward to where Mary was shaving a shrunken figure across the room. She did not know he was there until he spoke.

"What are you doing in Gopher?"

Patch was watching, curious to witness the meeting between these two and yet feeling an intruder, then he realized that Lindsay Stewart had also stopped and turned.

The girl almost slashed the cheek beneath her hand. She straightened, swinging around, still holding the straight razor expertly.

"Clint." Her smile went wide and her glance flicked over him. "Clint, you're all right. You look fine."

"Why wouldn't I be all right?" The words were a growl; the usually laughing man was not laughing now. "You've got no business to be here. Why did that idiot doctor let you leave Goldfield anyhow?"

She shook her head quickly. "He didn't want me to come. He forbade it, but I came anyway."

"Well, you're not staying. And you're

wasting your time shaving that scarecrow. He'll be dead by tomorrow."

"Clint."

He whirled away from her and hunched his shoulders, coming like a huge bear toward Adam Patch. For the first time, Adam realized that the man was very drunk. It did not tell in his motions, in his walk, but his breath was heavy with whiskey, his eyes not quite in focus and his words slurred when he spoke to Patch. He kept walking as if he would run Patch down, but the doctor held his position, and finally Clint stopped, almost touching the other. He planted his feet widely and thrust his chin forward.

"Ain't you got any sense at all?"

Adam Patch's temper was not the most docile in the world. The Irish in him was dominant and brooked little challenge, but he held himself in check now, saying in a level voice,

"This is not a place to quarrel, Clint. You're drunk."

"So I'm drunk." Collins raised a big hand and wiped it across his eyes as if to clear a blur. "Stay on the subject. Why'd you bring my wife to a place like this? You want her to get the fever?"

Lindsay Stewart was standing at one side. His voice came so low that Patch barely heard him. Certainly it did not carry across to the girl standing frozen where Collins had left her.

"Get out of here, you fool."

Collins twisted like a bull that finds it has more than one tormentor. "Keep clear of this, lawyer man."

"Touch me," said Lindsay Stewart, "and I'll kill you. I'd welcome the chance."

Collins stared at him in surprise, then suddenly he seemed to be more sober. Stewart's reputation with a gun was too well known to be ignored.

"This isn't your business."

Stewart spoke with contempt. "You are now in a hospital, and you're disturbing the patients, interfering with the doctor and bothering the nurse. Get out."

Collins gaped down at the smaller man, then he started to laugh, not a pleasant sound, but harsh and ugly. "That's a hot one. Nurse! She's my wife and I have the right to tell her what to do."

"Not when you're in this condition you don't."

"Please." Unnoticed by any of them Mary Collins had run forward to stop before Clint, peering anxiously up into his distorted face. "Please, Clint, you don't know what you're doing."

"Oh, yes I do."

She took his arm. "No. Listen to me. Doctor Patch tried to keep me from coming. So did Mr. Stewart."

He made a sudden sweeping gesture with his hand, breaking her grip and sending her stumbling backward to fall across one of the newly cleansed beds.

Lindsay Stewart moved with the sharp precision of a striking snake. His hand, looking incredibly small around the grip of the heavy gun, brought it from the holster in a flowing swing.

Patch thought he would shoot the miner instantly, and yelled, jumping forward to prevent it. But Stewart's arm continued up in an even arc and the gun barrel cracked against the curve of Collins' jaw, breaking the skin. Collins staggered back and Stewart was after him with the speed and coordination of a panther. This time the long barrel crashed down on the side of Collins' head.

Clint Collins' knees buckled and he went down, and Patch seized the lawyer as Stewart was again stepping in to deliver the finishing blow. For an instant Stewart struggled in Patch's grasp, but the doctor's grip held fast and Stewart subsided, finally saying in a roughened tone,

"You'd better let me put him out. He'll be far less trouble to us all."

Collins fumbled to his feet unsteadily, his chin bleeding and his eyes hot with anger. He glared at them each in turn, then turned and charged out of the building.

Stewart did not wait to see him leave. Already he was moving toward the girl. But before he could reach her, Mary Collins had found her feet. Then she was running, out into the dark street, calling Clint Collins' name.

Moments later she came back, her hair a nest for a hundred sparkling snowflakes. "I can't find him," she said desperately. "I don't know what to do."

Stewart had holstered his gun but his voice still held an edge. "Don't worry about him, the cold air will do him good."

She looked from Patch to Stewart and back to Patch, as if the doctor would offer more sympathy. "I never saw him act like that before."

"He's just drunk," Patch said softly, trying to quiet her.

She shook her head vigorously. "He's been drunk before, but never like this. He's usually so good humored. He never picks fights."

"He's scared." There was contempt again

in Stewart's tone. "He's trying to fight off the fever by crawling into a bottle. Forget him. He'll go someplace and sleep it off, if he doesn't sober up first."

She walked uncertainly to the door, peering out into the tumbling white screen. Patch lowered his voice and told Stewart,

"Maybe you'd better go locate him."

"Hell with him," Stewart growled. "I hope he freezes."

Patch's eyes narrowed and his tone was hardly a whisper. "You're really in love with her?"

For a single instant, fury flashed through the lawyer's eyes, and Adam Patch realized how very dangerous this small man could be. Then Stewart thrust his emotion down, hid it, and said in a controlled voice,

"There are certain questions that not even a physician is privileged to ask."

He spun on his small heel and went back to the medicine table.

Patch looked after him, then moved to the door and out, saying, as he passed the girl, "I've called a meeting at the store. I'll try to find Clint if you'll keep an eye on things until I get back."

She murmured a word of thanks and Patch headed down the dark street. It was snowing harder now, a blinding curtain of large, soft flakes that swirled and danced in the sharp downdraft, and the wind beat against his shoulders, his upturned collar.

Only two buildings showed light, and light was all that he could see of them. The store was one, the hotel the other. A lamp burned in its lobby and sent out a diffused glow to guide him. He plowed past it. Already there were four inches of snow on the ground. He hoped that it would not last through the night, thinking of the trouble his packers would have, even with their snowshoes.

He did not see the figure that detached itself from the hotel porch until they practically ran into each other. Then he heard Clint Collins' voice saying,

"I've been waiting, Doctor."

Immediately the man's fist slammed against his head, the surprise as much as the blow knocking him heavily to the slippery ground. His whole inclination was to stay there. His head rang from the force of the blow and the weariness that had been building through the last three days flowed over him in rhythmic waves.

It was the kick in the side that actually roused him, for Collins swung his huge booted foot against Patch's rib cage, bringing a sharp stabbing pain.

It brought him up out of the snow, gasping, as Collins charged. He managed to duck the roundhouse swing and clip the man a slicing blow on the chin.

Collins slipped in the snow and fell, going down hard enough to knock his breath out in an audible grunt. Patch did not know how much of the fall was accidental, how much due to his connecting fist, how much due to the pistol whipping Collins had taken from Lindsay Stewart. But it gave him time, while the bigger man was climbing up, to set himself.

He used his right to the jaw, his left to the stomach. Then as Collins staggered back, Patch was all over him, sending one blow after another against the hard jaw.

When it was finished, when the miner was down, Patch walked on to the store, taking time to steady his breathing. He walked in to find nearly a hundred people jammed in the warm room, waiting for him.

Sam Dohne was at the door and Patch nodded toward the street.

"Send a couple of men after Clint Collins. He's down, in the street in front of the hotel."

Silence hit the room like a cut switch. Dohne's eyes jumped.

"Fever?"

"Whiskey," said Adam Patch, "and a

couple of rights to his jaw." He held up his hand. The knuckles were red and blood seeped from one of them.

An audible sigh ran through the room. Patch looked up at the faces turned toward him. They were haunted faces, fearful faces, but at the moment they were touched with awe. Gopher was a tough camp, and Clint Collins was the strongest man in it; until now.

CHAPTER SEVEN

Leadership rises out of strength and fear. Both of these were working for Adam Patch as he faced the people assembled in the store.

The news that he had licked Clint Collins in a fight impressed the hardest criminal present, and the fact that he was a doctor who might therefore save them from the dreaded fever made them listen to him with double attention.

In the long board-and-batten room were some eighty men and three women. Patch's single glance identified the women for what they were, and a camp like Gopher did not attract the so-called good women of the world.

One, he saw, was older than the other two.

Her hair was dyed a purple-red. From this and from the jewelry she wore about her neck and wrists he appraised her as the madam. He chose her to talk directly to.

It was an old trick, one he had learned in medical school. You picked one person when talking to a crowd. You watched his reaction and learned from this whether you were getting your message across.

His voice was cold, his words purposely stinging. He did not care whether they liked him, only that they would obey him. And he wanted it understood from the very first that he would brook no disobedience. As long as the epidemic lasted, he intended to be boss of the camp.

"Most of you aren't much good."

His curt words came out like bullets from a Gatling gun. "I'm not going to pretend that I like you or that I put much trust in you. I recognize a number of you who are wanted in other camps. That's your business. I am not an officer of the law. But I'll put up with no foolishness. I'm going to lay down certain rules. They'll be obeyed. This is for the good of us all, for if they aren't followed most of us will die."

He paused, still watching the woman's face. It was a puffy face, bloated with years of too much rich food, too much strong drink, too many excesses.

"First, the girls are out of business for the time being. I have other uses for them. If there is one of you who will not nurse the sick, she can leave with the Indians in the morning. Understood?"

The woman met his eyes squarely. She did not answer, but she did nod her hennaed head, and he could tell by her expression that she accepted the order. He turned from her to center his attention on Kid Beale, for in the small killer he recognized a power to stand against him if Beale so chose.

"Next, those who have already had the fever and recovered, hold up your hands."

Nine hands came up, Beale's included.

"You will have charge of burials. You will have charge of changing the hospital beds and handling the patients. I'll divide you into three shifts, each to work eight hours."

He made the divisions, and got a nod from Beale when he named him captain of the details. He felt better with these two groups under control, but there was a long way to go before he would know that the camp was in his hands. He covered the hall with a sweep of his arm.

"All the rest of you stay out of the hospital. If you see someone fall sick, don't touch him. Contact somebody who has already had the fever. Is that understood?"

Still they nodded, as if only too glad to drop onto this doctor's shoulders the mantle of responsibility.

He swung abruptly to face Sam Dohne, raising his tone so that no one present could possibly miss his words. "From now on, until the fever is finished, there will be no drinking."

The murmur of protest rose then, and suddenly he was savagely angry. "I just told you that I don't like any of you, but I am here to help you. I will be obeyed. The first man I catch drunk, I will run out of camp into the mountains.

"And as for you," he leveled a long finger on Sam Dohne, "I'll hold you personally accountable. If there is any drinking, I'll have every whiskey keg in the place broken."

He left them then, timing his move to take advantage of the shocked silence of their surrender. He strode back up the steep, dark street, the quickness of his pace belying the bone-deep weariness that threatened to engulf him, and came into the improvised hospital to see Lindsay Stewart and Mary Collins sitting quietly beside the low-turned lamp near the corner stove.

They looked around sharply as Patch entered, and Stewart got slowly to his feet.

"How did it go?"

Adam Patch's shrug was more expressive than words. "All right, I think. It's a strange thing, Lindsay. Practically every man in this camp is a criminal of sorts, yet with the chips down they'll close ranks and pull together. Even the girls are going to help. Two will be here in a few minuts to relieve us. We all need sleep after that walk."

Mary Collins said softly, "Did you find Clint?"

"I did." Patch nodded and his tone was grim. He held up his bruised knuckles in silent explanation. "Your husband is cracking up, Mary. There's no use trying to fool you. You can see it for yourself."

Her only answer was a worried, low-drawn breath.

"The best thing I can think of is to get him out of here. I'll have to think about it and make a decision in the morning."

She still said nothing, and Patch knew that Lindsay Stewart was watching him.

"How are the patients?"

Stewart said, "They all seem to be asleep. At least there haven't been any new ones since you left."

Patch nodded, leaving them to walk around the room, pausing at each bed. Automatically he took the pulses, noted the flushed color of the faces in the yellow light of the lamp he had brought with him. Some seemed on the mend, but others had worsened. He shivered in a quick spasm. With the windows open and the wind bringing in its breath of snow the room was chill.

He had barely finished, when noise at the door drew his attention, and he saw the two girls step uncertainly inside. One was tall and blond with finely chiseled features that had not yet coarsened. Patch judged her to be very young, surely under twenty, and his curiosity was stirred despite his natural cynicism.

What had brought her to this desolate mountain camp? What story lay behind the deep sadness of the large blue eyes?

The second woman was older, perhaps thirty, dark, with a dumpy body that had thickened around the hips and waist. Patch glanced toward Mary Collins, trying to gauge her reaction. Few women of her class would accept this situation easily, but she had risen and was coming forward, holding out her hand.

"Hello. I'm Mary Collins."

He felt a rush of admiration for her poise, her naturalness. Both of the girls had stopped, both were eying her with open suspicion. Then the blonde gingerly touched the outstretched hand and said in a barely audible whisper,

"I'm Lily Meyer."

The older woman's tone was deeper. "Annie Lee." She, too, touched Mary Collins' fingers, but dropped her eyes as she did so until they focused on the boards of the splintered floor.

"Thank you for coming." Mary Collins' voice was warm and friendly. "It takes a lot of courage to nurse the fever. Come, and I'll show you what needs doing."

She led them away, talking easily, and Stewart and Patch looked at each other.

"She's quite a person." Patch was speaking more to himself than to Stewart.

"To be married to a drunken oaf." Stewart sounded furious, and his anger held him rigid as he stalked out into the night.

Patch looked after him, feeling a wash of sorrow for the little man. Lindsay Stewart had conquered his world, but here he had come up against something more important to him than all the court cases he had ever tried, and he was beaten before he began.

Adam turned back to see Mary Collins crossing toward him. Behind her, the two girls were already beginning to prepare themselves for their new tasks.

Mary in a low tone, "They're not afraid. I

think they will be all right."

"I'm sure of it," said Patch. "Now, you'd better go to the hotel and get some rest." He raised his voice to the girls. "If you want me, if there is another patient, I'll be at the hotel."

He watched them a moment, seeing them nod to him, and heard Mary Collins say in surprise,

"Why, where is Mr. Stewart?" She sounded as if she had just realized that the lawyer was no longer in the building.

"He was tired, I guess." Patch looked back at her. Her eyes showed him that she did not believe this, that she sensed something more than tiredness had sent Stewart away, but she did not speak. He tucked a hand beneath her arm and steered her to the door.

Outside the wind caught them with breath-taking force. It nearly swept the girl from her feet, and left her gasping. Patch hooked his arm about her waist and together they forged toward the hotel, their heads bowed, the heavy snowfall nearly blinding them.

The girl was shivering before they came into the bare, unpainted lobby. A single stand lamp burning on the end of the high desk managed only to enlarge the shadows lurking like waiting shrouds in the corners of the small room. The gust that came in with them through the open door sent the lamp flickering, almost extinguishing the smoky flame, and Patch put his shoulder to the door, forcing it closed, saying to the trembling girl,

"I don't know which room is mine."

"Ten," she said against the chatter of her teeth. "I was with Mr. Stewart when he had your gear brought in."

There was a keyboard behind the desk. Patch went around, lifting the large brass key from its hook, turning to look inquiringly at his companion.

She shook her head. "We're in Nine, but the key's gone. Clint must already be in bed."

They moved back along the hall together and paused before her door. The rising gale shook the frail building suddenly, rattling the windows and seeming about to collapse the pole walls.

She shivered again. "I hate wind."

"Nature," said Adam Patch, "is seldom gentle. Get some sleep, Mary. If the storm lets up you'll have a hard day tomorrow. I'm sending you back to town."

She didn't argue and he watched her go, seeing the resolute set of her small shoulders. Then he turned in to his own room.

It was narrow and cell-like, for floor space was at a premium in the canyon cleft. There was a single window against which snow had drifted until it was entirely shrouded. He saw this first in the flare of the match which he struck to light the oil lamp. His breath made a fluffy pattern as he turned to look at the lumpy bed, at the cracked pitcher, deliberately left dry since any water left in it might well have frozen.

And then he heard voices and was an unwilling eavesdropper for the wall between the two rooms was of single boards, covered only by canvas. Clint Collins sounded irritated and sullen, an awakened bear.

"So you decided to come to bed finally."

Adam Patch missed Mary's reply, her voice being too low to carry distinctly, but he heard Collins say quickly,

"What's this about leaving?"

"In the morning," she told him. "The doctor is sending us back to town."

"The doctor is sending us?" Collins' voice came up to a near roar. "Who in hell does he think he is to be sending us anywhere?"

"Shhh. He'll hear you. He's in the next room."

"And how do you know what room he's in?"

"Clint, please."

"Clint, please. Don't you Clint please me. I saw the way you looked at him. I saw the way you followed him up here. How often have you been seeing him in Goldfield?"

She slapped him then, the sound of the blow clearly heard through the partition. Patch swung toward his door. He heard her gasp and guessed that Collins had struck her in return. Then he had his door open and was in the hall.

But he was not the first there. In the shadowed light from the lobby he saw Lindsay Stewart's small form already outside the door of Nine, saw the lawyer push the panel open and realized that he had a gun in his hand.

He called sharply and got no response. Either Stewart failed to hear or chose not to. When Patch reached the entrance the girl half sat, half lay across the rumpled bed, the mark of a fresh bruise bright on her cheek.

Clint Collins stood above her. It was as if he had been about to seize her when the door burst open. He wore long, heavy underwear and his bare feet looked incredibly large. His head was turned and he was staring at Stewart with the look of a hypnotized bird held immobile by a snake.

"Don't." The word came out of him with

an explosive rush as he read his death in Stewart's face.

The lawyer's voice was utterly expressionless. "Walk out into the hall. Move."

It was then that Adam Patch seized him from behind, wrapping his long arms about the smaller man, grabbing the wrist and forcing it down until the gun's muzzle pointed at the floor.

He had expected Stewart to struggle. The lawyer did not, but Clint Collins, seeing him held powerless, jumped forward to drive one fist and then another into Stewart's face.

The lawyer slumped, a dead weight in Patch's arms, and the gun clattered from his nerveless fingers. From the bed, the girl cried out a wordless protest.

Collins was already diving for the gun and Patch threw the unconscious figure against him, himself stooping to retrieve the fallen weapon. The collision took Collins to the floor and Patch moved in swiftly, grabbing the gun before Collins could free himself and struggle to his feet. He held it loosely as the big man rose to stand glowering uncertainly at the doctor, breathing noisily through his nose.

"Get dressed."

Collins' expression turned to rebellion. "Go to hell."

Patch took a quick step forward, balancing the gun. "Get your clothes on. I'm going to send Jake Longstreet and the Indians down the canyon in the morning. Jake will establish a quarantine camp at the wagons and wait two weeks. If no one comes down with the fever in that time he will go on to Goldfield."

"What's that got to do with me?"

"You're going with him, and you're staying with him. I've enough on my hands here without worrying about you."

Collins jerked his head toward his wife. "What about her?"

"She stays here. I was going to send her out with you, but she's safer with the fever."

"So that's the way it is." Collins' mouth was ugly. "I'll kill you, Doc."

"Maybe," said Patch, "but you might get hurt trying." He waved the gun slightly. "The choice is yours, Clint. I'm not as softhearted as Stewart. I won't even bother taking you into the hall before I shoot."

Clint Collins blinked into Patch's hard eyes. Then slowly, without another word, he began to put on his clothes.

Stewart was stirring. Stewart sat up slowly. He stared at the big miner, then at Patch beside the door still balancing the gun. He rose slowly, the bruises on his jaw showing

89

plainly, but he did not speak. There were times when Lindsay Stewart had the sense to keep his mouth shut.

Collins was finished finally. He looked at his wife for the first time since Patch had entered the room. He glanced at Patch. Then with a single snort he stalked past the doctor and down the hall. Patch followed. They crossed the lobby in complete silence and bent into the bitter night.

CHAPTER EIGHT

Patch's hospital had three fresh cases the following morning, and two of the previous patients had died during the night. Adam Patch stood surveying the room, knowing the weight of hopelessness.

Of necessity a doctor must recognize that a percentage of his patients will die, more than necessary when they do not consult him until an extremity forces them to. But to be faced with a creeping death that struck blindly and without warning, a death which it seemed nothing would arrest, was a challenge outside his experience. He watched automatically as the women moved in their silent ritual, bathing the patients under Mary Collins' direction. He watched Mary follow them, shaving and comforting those who had been washed, and he marveled at her composure.

He had not spoken to her directly since escorting her husband to the Indians' camp. By now, he assumed that Collins was well down the canyon. The snow had stopped before daylight, but the driving wind continued and the powdery whiteness swirled between the drab buildings like the trailings of an angry ghost, so filling the air that it was difficult to see.

He breathed deeply, filling his lungs despite the fact that the air in the big room was heavy with the thick odor of sickness. It seemed to have a body that the wind through the windows did not blow away, nor the chill of the snow freeze off. In Tonopah, he had heard, the cold had finally killed the fever, but here it seemingly had no power to stop the epidemic.

He shook his head, trying to shake off his depression, and went forward to where Mary Collins was working over a thin, dark-haired man. A puckered knife scar ran from the corner of the slitlike mouth up to the tail of the eyebrow. Patch recognized Scarface Boyer, wanted in Tonopah for the causeless killing of three helpless Chinese, and his lips quirked a little in self-irony. Here he was, ninety miles from his comfortable rooms, enduring the rigors of the mountain camp, to save the life of a man who justly should hang.

And Mary Collins, bending over, the certain strokes of her razor cleansing the scarred cheek, should not be called upon to touch such a creature.

It hurt him, the idea that she must do a menial job for a murderer. He had never experienced this feeling before. A nurse's job was to nurse, and there were many unpleasant duties connected with it. Why should he care what Mary Collins did or did not do? But he did care. He knew it suddenly. This woman had more attraction for him than any he had ever known.

He stood, trying to analyse himself. He had been very certain that he was in love with Clara Holister. But exactly what did the word love mean to him? It meant many things to different people. It was related to all of the emotions: pity, protectiveness, even to hate.

He knew in this moment that a part of Clara's attractiveness had been the social position she occupied. If Goldfield boasted a society, her family was near the top. And he had been aware of his own beginnings, of the ridiculous figure that his small, pompous, strutting father made.

Many of the people he had gone to school with were of the leading Eastern families, and he had admired their sisters and their friends for the poise that good breeding had given them. It came as a belated understanding that Mary Collins possessed this same poise, this ease of manner and certain balance. Where she had gotten it he had no way of knowing, but have it she did. He recalled a phrase that his mother had used. A lady is born, not made.

It was another unhealthy train of thought, he knew, and on impulse moved toward the hennaed woman he had singled out the night before and said in a low voice:

"I didn't get your name."

She pulled the cover over her finished patient, dried her hands and straightened, facing him with a show of defiance.

"I'm Maggy South."

His glance sharpened on her. In her own way, this woman was as famous as any of the gunmen who had drawn their flaming records across the frontier.

She had been in Virginia City, in White Pine, in Denver and Central City, and, in the curious hybrid society that had ruled the lawless camps, hers had been a voice to reckon with.

She saw his look and her heavily painted

mouth twisted in a derisive line.

"You're Doc Patch's boy. I've known your pa for a long time."

She nodded, relaxing at his smile. "And you're wondering what I'm doing in a hell-hole like Gopher."

"It doesn't seem to make good sense."

She gave him a snorting laugh. "Nothing in this crazy life makes much sense, Doc. Don't ask me why people do what they do. Don't ask me why women like me fall for a man's promises. Hell, we look on men as suckers, someone to take money from, to roll when they're drunk, to put up with because we have to. So I listened to Sam Dohne."

His disbelief at this possibility showed in his eyes, and her laugh was a low, wicked thing, as cutting as a scalpel.

"Our kind are suckers, always. Why else do you think the girls put up with their cadets, support them, take the beatings from them, give them most of our money?"

He spread his hands, listening.

"Because every human being needs some-one who belongs to him. I've known Sam Dohne for years. No one ever has come closer to a hanging he deserved. But he's a man and he's got a line of talk that's conned money out of people a lot smarter than I am." She paused. "So he needed capital. He came to me, I backed him in this mine, but I don't trust him. I came up to see that I get my share."

Patch's smile widened. "Then you own part of that ball of gold?"

"It was my idea. I heard the toughs talking at the house. It was the only way I figured we could save it."

Patch laughed aloud. He found himself liking Maggy South. There was a fundamental honesty about her that broke through the crust of her embittering experiences. She would, he thought, rob a man with one hand and nurse him back to health with the other.

"You'll have fewer thieves to worry about now, with those the fever's taking gone and those who went down the trail with Indian Jake this morning. How many did leave?"

She grunted. "About a dozen. No-goods. Loafers."

Patch caught the censure in her tone. "But the girls all stayed, didn't they, Maggy?"

Her head came up straight on the thick neck and her shoulders went back, thrusting forward the full bosom, but her voice was mocking.

"Sure they stayed. What good is a dead man to them?" She swaggered off, picked up the used pan of foul water and carried it away to change it. Then she bore down like a ship under full sail upon the next prone and burning man.

Mary Collins finished shaving the scar-faced killer and also went for clean water. As she turned, she saw Patch for the first time that morning. She hesitated, and color came into her cheeks.

"Good morning."

He nodded, watching her move on. She carried the basin to the slop pail beneath the shelf which held the medicines, and emptied it, refilling it from the big kettle which boiled on the stove. Finally she faced him as if she realized that she could no longer put off a conversation that was bound to be painful.

"I haven't thanked you for last night."

He shrugged it away, embarrassed because he knew that she was embarrassed. "Those things happen, Mary."

"He's so changed. He never was that way before."

"He's frightened," said Patch. "I wonder that he didn't take off from here before."

"It's the gold. That horrible ball of gold. He's afraid that if he leaves, he'll never get any part of it. He's like all the other men in this camp. They're afraid of the fever but

96

their greed is stronger than their fear."

Patch knew that she was right. But at least he had Clint Collins off his neck. He made the rounds of the beds and then went back to the hotel in search of breakfast.

The first man he saw when he walked into the long, narrow dining hall was Clint Collins. The big man sat at the far end of the stained table, eating as if he felt that this was his last meal on earth.

Collins looked up as Patch stopped in the doorway, and his heavy lips twisted into what was for him a smile of mockery.

"Morning, Doc. How's all the dead ones?"

There were four other men at the table. One was Kid Beale, and Patch caught the shadow of annoyance that crossed the small killer's face. He ignored the others. He walked the length of the table slowly until only feet separated him from Collins.

"How did you get loose from Longstreet?"

Collins smirked. "He ain't so sharp any more, Doc. I just waited until he went to sleep and walked out."

"Just walk back. You'll find them with the wagons."

"Make me." Collins rose quickly until he towered above Patch. His eyes glittered with an inner hunger of all-consuming rage, and Patch realized that the man had been sitting here, waiting for his arrival, planning his scene in advance.

It was one thing to handle Collins when he was drunk, when his timing was off, his eyes uncertain, his legs unsteady. It was quite another to give away forty pounds and three inches. And the fact remained, he simply could not afford to let Clint Collins whip him.

He knew that the men at the table were watching for his reaction, that what he did here in this room at this moment might well determine whether he stayed in control of this camp or not.

And it was imperative that he did maintain control, for, if the epidemic continued and men's panic grew, Gopher would degenerate into a state of hysteric anarchy.

"I'm not going to make you leave." He said it evenly. "You're the one who is coming apart at the seams. If you haven't the sense to get out when you have the chance, stay here and die." He walked away and took a chair at the table, hearing Kid Beale laugh as he passed.

Clint Collins glared at him wordlessly. He shifted his feet as if he meant to come after Patch, then checked himself. He had expected an argument. He had been yearning for a fight, to take out on the smaller man the fear and frustration which had him in its grasp. But as the seconds ticked off, the resolve drained out of him. It was hard to sustain anger when your opponent utterly ignored you.

A down-shouldered man shuffled in from the kitchen, a none too clean apron tied across his bulging middle. He did not ask Patch what he wanted. He brought a plate of fried salt meat, of beans, and a plate of sour-dough biscuits.

The others had all turned their attention back to their food, also ignoring Collins, and suddenly the miner turned with a muttered oath and stomped through the kitchen door.

Kid Beale said in a dry voice, "The sand's running out of his craw."

A man at his elbow, whom Patch did not know, laughed shortly. "There never was much to begin with."

No one else spoke. One by one they finished their plates and left the room until Adam Patch was alone at the table.

He ate the greasy mess and leaned back, finding a cigar in his coat pocket and lighting it carefully, obsessed by the need for action yet knowing that there was nothing he could do that he had not already done.

Only time would tell how soon the sickness could be checked. He rose and crossing the deserted lobby came again into the street.

The snow had started again, tiny icy particles that cut against his cheeks as he plowed toward the store through the mounting drifts. If this storm held for another twenty-four hours, the stricken camp would surely be snowbound.

The storeroom was crowded and he frowned. It would have been far better if these people had stayed as widely separated as possible, but there was another facet to consider. As a group, they might bolster each other's courage; alone, they would suffer from the numbing fear that wrapped the camp.

Sam Dohne came forward when he saw Patch, and pulled him into a far corner behind a pile of blankets on the low wooden counter. The man's thick face was a picture of worry and his tone had a hangdog whine.

"That Clint Collins. He was in here and filled a jug. I tried to stop him. Honest I did, Doc, but he just laughed at me."

Adam Patch's face hardened. "Where is he now?"

"He went up to the mine. I told him what you said about busting the whiskey barrels and he just laughed. He said to tell you that the next time you came for him you'd better be wearing a gun and you'd better be ready to use it."

CHAPTER NINE

The tunnel which was the adit to the Gopher Mine sloped out of the steep canyon wall a good thousand feet above the twisting main street of the storm-beaten town.

Even in good weather it would have been a fearsome climb, and with the wind-whipped snow filling the crevasses and drifting across the trail it was one to make any man hesitate.

Clint Collins' huge tracks were already nearly obscured as Adam Patch started his struggle upward. He cursed himself as he climbed. The camp below needed his attention, and he certainly felt no love for Collins.

But the girl was different. She clung to the big man no matter what he did, and Patch had seen her face when she had heard the news. Kid Beale had come to the hospital on his shift to carry out the dead. He had commented on the smell of the whiskey Patch was using as an antiseptic, saying that the only healthy man who had any was Clint Collins, who was drunk and had headed for the mine where the fool would probably go

101

to sleep and freeze to death.

Certainly a man could well freeze in this weather. The cold bit through Patch's blanket coat although he was sweating beneath his heavy clothes from the exertion of the climb.

He stumped doggedly on. The narrow, shelflike road that had been hacked out of the rock face for the passage of the small ore wagons, was barely discernible beneath the white cover.

He never afterward knew how long the climb took him, but when he finally crested out over the breast of the snow-softened dump he was perilously near the point of exhaustion.

The head frame stood like a gaunt specter, snow clinging to its rough surface, marking the entrance to the slanting haulage tunnel. Beside it rose the toolhouse, where Clint might have gone, but Patch chose the tunnel knowing that it would be warmer inside.

He staggered into the entrance and groped slowly back, his hands on the sharp rock of the wall, his feet stumbling over the crossties which held the slender iron rails in place.

Suddenly it was eerily quiet around him. He stopped; his mind, sluggish with his tiredness, taking time to realize that the mountain had cut out the howl of the driving storm. He shook himself and pushed onward. The tunnel rose at an almost imperceptible grade. It was built so purposely, so that gravity could help in bringing out the ore cars heavy with their loads of broken ore. But Patch was so weary that even this small incline made walking twice as difficult.

He fumbled ahead. It was cool in the tunnel but, after the harsh cold outside, the air felt warm to his chilled face. He progressed a hundred yards into the darkness, unthinking, before he unwillingly sank down to rest. He did not sleep but sat in a torpor, his mind numb, his reactions very slow.

Later, his natural resilience asserted itself and his chilled body gained warmth. He rose at last, recalling almost in surprise his reason for being in the mine. He stood hesitating, wondering if Collins were really in the tunnel. There was the possibility that the man had not reached the mine. Still, Patch had seen no indication that he had fallen from the trail on his way up even though his footprints had been filled and obliterated far below the dump. Patch could only assume that he had reached it, for if he had not, there was no hope of finding him now alive.

If he were somewhere underground he

was probably safely asleep, for there was no danger of freezing within the mountain. Patch was tempted to turn back, but he could not do so with no more assurance, than he had, to take to the girl.

He began again to move forward. He had no idea how long the adit was, and he had spent enough time underground to realize the danger of exploring an unknown tunnel without a light.

He jerked himself to more alertness, turned and made his way out to the entrance again.

Beyond it, the snow had stopped but the wind still whirled the powdery particles with endless fury. He forced open the door of the mine shack and found what he was looking for on a shelf to the right. A carbide lamp.

There was a can of carbide beneath the shelf. He filled the lamp and then, packing snow into the water container, he held a match under it until it melted. That done, he lit the resulting gas, fastened the lamp to his hat and made his way back along the tunnel at a more rapid rate.

There was no timbering. The rock stood firm with no sign of slippage, and the tunnel had been driven high enough for him to walk erect without bending his head. Whatever faults Sam Dohne had, the man was an experienced miner and it showed in his work.

Clint Collins was at the face. There was a single jack beside him, and the iron bit projected from the hole he had been drilling. The jug of whiskey was close to his left hand. Patch assumed that the liquor had overcome him and that he had fallen to the stone floor, extinguishing his lamp in his fall.

He stooped, grasping the bigger man's shoulder, meaning to shake him awake. Instead he turned Collins onto his back and stared down at a face which had reddened until it approached the color of purple.

Adam Patch was not a profane man, but he swore now. Clint Collins was drunk, yes, but he also had the fever. The signs were unmistakable. It had struck him down with the same suddenness that it felled all of its victims.

One moment Collins had been swinging the sledge, drilling the hole for the powder shot that would send the face crumbling into broken pieces of ore. The next instant he had dropped, to lie unmoving where he fell, in a deep stupor that might as well have been unconsciousness.

Patch straightened slowly. His mind was

freshly charged by the problem that now confronted him. It was a good half mile to the tunnel's mouth, and he doubted his ability to carry Collins any fraction of the distance.

An empty ore car stood on the shunted track ready to be filled after the shot was fired. Gratefully Patch wheeled it as close to the face as the track would permit and stooping, caught the sick man beneath both arms.

Collins weighed two hundred and sixty or seventy pounds against his own hundred and eighty-five, and it was dead weight. The sides of the ore car were some four feet above the ground level, and it took everything Patch had to drape the miner across them, his arms trailing on one side, his legs on the other.

The car ran down the grade nearly of its own weight. It required very little effort on Patch's part to get it moving, and had the wheels been perfectly round it would have coasted out of the mine alone. As it was, Patch walked behind it, giving it an occasional push when it hesitated at the bad rail joints, until they reached the entrance.

Here he stopped. It was out of the question that he carry Collins down the trail. But again he solved his difficulty, finding three boards in the mine shack, nailing crosspieces to bind them together and shaping them into a crude sled.

He rolled the big, limp figure onto this, attached a rope around Collins' chest to check the sled's natural progress, and began the tortuous trip down the narrow shelf to the town far below.

The descent took him an hour. Twice, the sled lodged in drifts. Once Collins rolled from it and nearly went over the edge of the trail where the ground dropped sharply for two hundred sheer feet.

Patch was again chilled through by the time he came down the last slanting loop and into Gopher's main street. Every muscle he owned ached in protest and he feared that the sick man might have frozen in spite of his fever-heated body, but when he pulled off his glove and touched Collins' cheek he found it still too hot.

He straightened, looking in concern down the snowy, empty length of the road. A hump interrupted the grade and he doubted that at this time he could drag the sodden sled over it.

Then Sam Dohne and Kid Beale appeared from the hotel. Patch waved to them, yelling, but even as he yelled, he knew that the wind was whipping the words to quick silence. In hopelessness he stopped his voice.

But they saw him, and then were hurrying forward. Kid Beale caught the sled rope from his stiffened fingers and together they turned toward the hospital.

Mary Collins bent above one of the rear beds. She looked up as they came in, saw that Beale and Patch were carrying a man between them and moved quickly to an empty bed, turning back the covers in preparation.

"Another one." Her voice sounded tired, almost despairing as though the duties of the day were piling too heavily upon her shoulders.

And then she realized who they carried and her voice changed, roughened, as she unconsciously fought for control.

"Clint!"

Patch and Beale laid the stricken man on the bed. The doctor began at once to strip the heavy clothing from his burning body, talking as he worked.

"Get a cool sponge ready. Keep him damp for a while. That may lower the fever. Get some whiskey on that cut." He had uncovered a gash on the shoulder that the man must have suffered in his roll from the sled.

Kid Beale eased in, shoving Patch aside.

"Let me, Doc. There's no use you taking more chances than necessary. We need you."

Patch stepped back, glad of the chance for momentary rest, thinking as he watched how much Beale had changed. It was hard, seeing him treat Collins as tenderly as if the big man were a baby, to remember that he was a cold-blooded, ruthless killer.

Beale spoke without turning as Mary Collins hurried back with the cool water and cloths, the whiskey.

"Doc, why'n't we pour a little of that liquor down his throat? It might shock him awake."

"No." Patch shook his head. "It would only heat him further. He's too hot now. But get some water down him if you can. The best chance is to let him sweat. Wash him off and then cover him, and keep doing it."

Mary Collins' eyes were wide on her husband's flushed face. "Where did you find him?"

"In the mine tunnel. He'd been working, drilling for a shot in the face. Apparently he dropped suddenly, like all the rest."

"Thank you. If you hadn't made that terrible climb, we would never have found him in time."

At the back of his mind Patch was not at

all certain that they had found Clint Collins in time, but he saw nothing to be gained by saying so.

"It's all right."

"It isn't all right. It isn't fair." Her tone gained a note of violence that he had not heard there before. "Clint acted like a fool. If he'd gone with Jake this morning. . . ."

"It wouldn't have made any difference," Patch told her. "He already had the fever, Mary. We don't know how many days it takes to develop, but certainly it is not overnight. At best he would have fallen in the trail. At worst he might have headed for Goldfield when he escaped Jake."

She answered with a nod and moved forward to assist Beale in undressing her husband, but when he was safely in the bed Beale pushed her aside also and began the sponging. Mary Collins turned back to Patch.

"Go to the hotel and rest. You need it. We can't afford to have you get sick."

He looked around the room. "How are things here?"

"Three new cases, not counting Clint. Two deaths."

He didn't answer. There was nothing he could say. He watched her wave her hands slightly in a small hopeless gesture, then go again to the bed and adamantly take the cloth from Beale.

"Let me care for him, Kid. He's my husband, and there are other jobs for you."

Kid Beale stepped back, touched Patch's arm and led him toward the door, and waited to follow him into the cold of the street.

Beale spat into the wind. "That was quite a haul you had, Doc." There was tinge of admiration in his voice that he had seldom showed for any man.

Patch shrugged. He was too tired to care about much of anything.

"He isn't worth it. He's a phony, a blow-hard, a four-flusher."

"He's sick," said Patch.

"Now that wife of his. There's an angel if anyone ever saw one. Every man in camp thinks so. How does a man like Clint Collins get a girl like that?"

"Why ask me?" Patch did not want to discuss Mary Collins with Kid Beale. He did not want to discuss her with anyone.

"I wasn't really asking," said Kid Beale. "I guess I was just kind of thinking aloud. A man had a girl like that, he could be about anything he wanted to."

Adam Patch looked down at the smaller man, at his thin, wolfish, cruel face, and he

111

wondered what the story was behind Beale, what circumstances had made him into what he was.

"Need a man depend on a woman, Kid?"

Beale shrugged. "A man has to depend on someone. If he hasn't got a woman, he has only himself." He plowed on through the snow, head down into the wind, heading for the store. Patch turned in at the hotel.

He crossed the empty lobby and moved along the silent hall toward his room. Inside, it was very chilly, the wind coming through the wall as if it were a sieve. He shucked out of his heavy coat, removed his boots which were soaked with snow, and, throwing back the thick blankets, stretched himself fully dressed upon the bed.

His head had hardly touched the pillow when he heard steps in the hall outside and a knock on his door. Without rising up he called,

"Come in."

The door opened and Lindsay Stewart stepped into the room. He shut the door carefully, precisely, as he did everything, and moved over to the bed, his thin-lipped mouth a slightly mocking line.

"I hear you just performed another heroic act."

Patch did not answer.

"Couldn't you let well enough alone? If the bum had died in the mine tunnel a lot of people would have been better off."

"Meaning yourself?"

Stewart's eyes showed their quick anger, then he laughed. "You ride people kind of hard, don't you, Doc? Meaning me, yes. Meaning Mary. The man's got no sand."

"Maybe he has something you don't. Maybe he's got kindness. Maybe he wouldn't wish someone had been left to die in a mine tunnel deliberately."

Stewart started to snort, then stopped and said in a careful tone, "You don't like me very well, do you, Doctor?"

"Let's say that I don't approve of you. I'm not too certain that Mary Collins would be any better off in your hands than she is in Clint's. I don't know him very well, and from what I've seen he is something of a blowhard and a bully. But he was kind to her when she needed help. He didn't take advantage where another man might."

"You believe I would have?"

"Look at yourself. You know yourself better than I do."

"I want to marry her."

"Now, sure. But would you have married her if you'd found her as Clint did, or would you have done what half the men up there were apparently trying to do?"

"Dammit," said Stewart, "you have a nasty way of putting things."

"Life has a nasty way of turning."

"You know damn well she'd be better off with me. I never in my life struck a woman."

"No," said Patch, and rolled over to face the wall, "but there are more subtle ways of torturing women than striking them. Make sure that if something happens to Clint Collins and she marries you that you keep this in mind."

There was silence behind him, then the shifting of feet on the bare-board floor, then the sound of the door opening and closing, again very softly.

CHAPTER TEN

It was still snowing as Adam Patch made his way along the dark street toward the hospital. There is something quiet about a snowy night, so quiet that the silence speaks to you. The wind had died and the flakes were larger, which meant that the temperature had moderated slightly.

It seemed to Patch that the snowfall would never cease. He waded through a drift which had formed during the afternoon, the thick whiteness reaching almost to his waist.

He hoped that the Indians and the quarantined had made it safely out, for the canyon trail below the town must by now be impassable.

How long it would last he could not guess. It was late in the year for such a heavy fall, but these high peaks carried snow well into the summer months. At the moment, the camp was as isolated as if it were located on the moon. There was little chance that anyone could leave now, however much they might want to.

He reached the hospital, went in and paused just inside the door to look at the long, dim room.

Mary Collins sat in a straight chair, motionless beside her husband's bed. The girl, Lily Meyer, worked at the rear, changing a bed, and aside from them there was no one else in the room except the bedded patients. Mary did not hear him until he came up behind her and spoke.

"Good evening."

She started, looking up and back, showing him a drawn face and tired eyes, but a smile touched the corner of her mouth and deepened the tiny dimple that occupied her cheek.

"Did you get some rest?"

"Enough. Have you had anything to eat?"

She shook her head. "Not yet."

He glanced at his watch. It was after eight. "You shouldn't have gone without for so long."

She said, "I didn't want to leave Lily by herself, and no one else has come."

"Where's Maggy South?"

She turned and pointed toward a bed in the corner.

"When?"

"She collapsed on the street this afternoon."

He crossed the room to pause beside the bed. Her bloated face now had a tinge of purple. He put his hand on her forehead and felt the burning skin, then he tested her pulse. It was very rapid, as if her heart were laboring at twice the normal speed.

He returned to Mary Collins, who had not moved, passed her and tested Clint Collins' pulse. It, too, was rapid and the face was very discolored, the lips parted and the breathing heavy. He let go of the wrist and turned away, and Mary Collins rose, saying quietly,

"He's worse."

"He's not any better. Go on, get your supper and some rest. Sleep if you can."

"I should stay."

"I'll be here."

"You can't stay all night."

"Do as I tell you."

She looked at him for a long moment as if she would refuse, then dropped her eyes and picking up her coat, disappeared through the doorway. Adam Patch gazed after her thoughtfully before he began to make his rounds. He paused first at the medicine table, noting how alarmingly low his supplies were running, then looked at the chart which Mary Collins was keeping.

Four more people had died during the day. Three new cases had been admitted. He stared at the paper. The writing on it was round, clear, almost juvenile. He thought that if handwriting was indicative of a person's character, it well told the story of Mary Collins.

She was as honest, as open as the wide loops of her careful script, but she did have a childlike quality of trustfulness that Patch had found to be rare among the women he had known.

He studied the information she had noted against each new entry. It told the patient's name, his point of origin if known, his employment, his nearest relative. Patch smiled a little cynically, wondering how much of the information she had so carefully noted was authentic. Most of these people had used so many names in their varying careers that they, themselves, no longer remembered the name they had had at the beginning of their lives.

At the bottom of the list was Maggy South. She was listed as forty-eight. He wondered where that information had come from, one of the girls probably. There was no stated birthplace, nor was there an occupation.

He heard sound behind him and turned to find Lily Meyer looking across his shoulder. For an instant their eyes met and again it startled him how very blue hers were.

"She going to die, Doc?" The voice was low-throated with a warm overtone.

"I don't know."

"Don't seem right. First decent thing she ever did in her life and she dies because of it."

"She probably had the fever coming on before she first walked in here."

He saw by her face that she did not believe him, and added, "If you're scared, Lily, go on back to the house."

"What's the use? If I'm going to get it, I've got it already. It don't matter anyhow."

There was such hopelessness in the voice that he was genuinely touched. She was so very young, and there was something definitely appealing about her. He thought savagely, This whole thing is beginning to get me. I'm going soft in the head. When I get sentimental about a streetgirl it's time I ran a check on myself.

Aloud he said, "Nothing is ever so bad that it can't mend, Lily. You don't have to stay with what you're doing."

"What else can I do, Doc? I've got no ability and there's not much for any woman to do in these towns."

"How old are you, Lily?"

"I'll be eighteen next week, if I live that long."

"You've got a good chance to make it." He grinned a little. "As good or better than most of us. It's a chance everyone takes, Lily. Don't start dying now, you're too young."

"You're a nice guy, Doc."

Patch was surprised. "And what makes you say that?"

"I don't know. I've seen lots of men. Mostly they're pigs. You ain't. You don't look at me the way they do, like I was dirt."

"I don't think you're dirt."

"But you think the way I make my living is wrong?"

"It's wrong for you if you have to ask that question. It bothers you, Lily."

She was silent, staring at him with her oversized eyes until he became nervous. Suddenly she said, "Do something for me, will you, Doc? Kiss me the way you'd kiss a decent woman? Kiss me the way you'd kiss Mrs. Collins if she wasn't married."

Shock ran through him. "What are you talking about?"

Her smile was apologetic. "I see the way you look at her. I know how you feel, even if you don't know yourself. It's part of my job to try to understand men. The trouble is, I understand what they're thinking much too well."

He reached out and took her slight shoulders with his big hands. He bent his head and kissed her gently, meaning for it to stop there. But suddenly her arm was around his neck and she was clinging to him like a drowning person who fights desperately for life. Her mouth was hot against his, her body pressed as tightly as possible into the curve of his own.

He returned the kiss instinctively. His arms tightened about her slender body, feeling the curving softness beneath the dress. Then he caught himself up and gently disengaged her.

"Not now, Lily."

She looked up at him and he was startled

to see the glint of tears in her large eyes. "I don't blame you."

He shook his head. "It isn't what you think, Lily." He hoped he was convincing. "I made a rule that as long as this sickness lasts there will be none of this. There's too much chance of spreading the fever."

She nodded slowly, not quite feeling rejected but also not quite sure.

He stepped away from her, making his voice brisk as he told her, "I'd better check on our patients."

His check was far from reassuring. Two of them were dead.

He came back to the girl, sending her down the snowy street in search of Kid Beale and the burial detail. Beale and two men arrived a few minutes later and silently carried the bodies off to be burned and buried.

Lily stood watching them without words, but her face held the haunting shadow of growing fear.

"When will it end, Doc?"

Patch shrugged. "Some of them are getting better now."

"What if everyone dies? What if I'm the last left?"

"I don't think everyone will."

"No, but what if everyone did and I was

the last one? I'd go crazy, Doc. I can't stand it."

She ran at him suddenly and threw both arms about his neck. "I mean it. I can't stand thinking about it."

"Everyone won't die." It was Mary Collins. She had come into the room without either of them seeing her.

Lily jumped backward, away from him, as if the floor beneath her feet had turned withering hot.

Patch felt a flush creep into his cheeks but he managed to keep his voice level.

"You should be asleep."

"I've had three hours. It's time Lily had some rest. Go ahead, child. I'll take over."

The girl looked at her and then at Patch as if for instructions. He nodded and without a word she reached for her coat and fled through the door.

Mary Collins said, "How's Clint?"

Patch did not answer the question. Instead he said, "What you saw was not what you may think it was."

Mary turned to look at him fully. "It doesn't matter, Doctor." She was more formal than he had ever heard her.

"It matters quite a lot." He saw the quick color rise in her face.

"Please."

"Listen," he said. "I'm not Lindsay Stewart, nor am I making any advances, but you are one of the most attractive women I have ever known. And you are in a situation that may get far more difficult before it gets better, if it ever gets better. I know that you would hesitate to go to Stewart for help. I'm only telling you that if you need help you can come to me without obligation or involvement."

She reached out strongly and put a hand on his arm. "Thank you, Adam. You don't know what that means to me."

"I think I do," he said. "If I didn't, I wouldn't have told you. People are so often foolish about these things. They bottle up their troubles inside and those troubles grow, where if they would bring them out into the open and discuss them thoroughly they could alleviate a great deal of misery. A doctor can be used as a clergyman. What is told to him is privileged."

"And you are asking me to talk to you openly?"

"I'm only saying that if you feel free to talk, it will be better for you."

She glanced around the room, and he understood her thought.

"There's nothing to do but wait, and waiting with death at your elbow is the hardest job in the world."

She came back and sat down in the straight chair beside the medicine table. "I'd like to talk about Clint," she said. She wasn't looking at Patch. Her eyes were on her hands knitted in her lap.

"Clint did so much for me and I feel that I failed him, and now that he really needs help there is nothing I can do."

"What makes you feel you failed him?"

"I never loved him the way he loved me. Maybe I'm not capable of loving anyone truly."

"The word love is one I'm afraid of," Patch told her. "It means so many different things to different people. Many make the mistake of taking the animal urge to get together, for love. Actually, I don't think sex has much to do with it."

"What does love mean to you?"

He considered carefully. "I don't know exactly. I think I would consider myself in love when the other person's happiness and well-being were more important to me than my own."

She shook her head slowly. "I've never felt that way toward anyone. I'm grateful to Clint. I feel guilty because I can't return the love he has for me. He does love me. He's proud of me. But he doesn't share his life with me, if you know what I mean. . . ."

She broke off, for a man had rushed through the door wide-eyed and gasping.

"Sam Dohne's got it. . . ." His voice cracked with the news. "He fell down in the middle of the store five minutes ago. Kid Beale is bringing him along now."

CHAPTER ELEVEN

The news that Sam Dohne was down fell like a pall across the whole camp. It was not that the old bull was well liked, for hardly a man in Gopher classed him as a friend. But there was something in Dohne's very ruggedness that had seemed to make him immune to the troubles that came to others. Half a dozen times he had escaped hanging by the skin of his teeth; he had been shot at, had run out of towns ahead of a posse, yet always survived.

But the fever had him now. All the following day, men crowded into the store to talk in hushed voices. Many who had thus far refused to leave because of the ball of gold now argued the possibility of fighting their way through the heavy snow pack, down to the quarantine camp at the foot of the mountain.

Adam Patch took time away from the

hospital to make a second speech in the store, threatening with slow torture any who went further than Jake Longstreet's camp, who carried the fever to the populous valley communities.

It had stopped snowing. The sky was blue and cloudless and innocent. The sun was out and its rays were blinding against the background whiteness.

Patch worked through the night and went to bed at five o'clock in the morning when Lindsay Stewart came to relieve him. He left Stewart and Mary Collins alone in the hospital, and as he walked through the cold morning darkness he wondered what they would talk about, and realized that he was jealous.

The girl Lily had been right, for in the few days since they had left Goldfield, Mary Collins had come to mean more to him than any woman he had ever known. He was still not certain that he was in love with her. He still shied away from the word. He was student enough of human relations to suspect that had they not been so closely thrown together in this short time the attraction might not exist.

But he knew that he would never stand by and let her return to Clint Collins without trying to prevent it.

He was bone tired and the bed closed about him and he slept, not coming awake until the afternoon sun had already dropped behind the canyon rim.

He rose then, made his way to the hotel kitchen and helped himself from the huge bean pot that the old cook had left simmering on the back of the range.

Noise at the door made him look that way and he found Lily standing hesitant, watching him. He nodded, carrying his plate to the table and sat down.

She said, "I'll get you some coffee," and crossed to take a cup from the rack, then go to the stove.

He watched her as she lifted the blackened pot, and speculated on what she would have been like if she had met the right man and married him. Seeing her in the kitchen, at the stove, somehow made her seem more womanly.

She wore a simple dress of wool, high collared and as demure as a kitchen apron, and the appealing quality he had noticed in the hospital was very strong. Had she been a tougher person, with her looks and this quality she could have sold herself in a market where women were at a premium. But she was not tough. No matter what her life had been, it was through weakness, not through strength.

He caught himself. He thought, It would be terribly easy to get involved with her. I could take her back to Goldfield and find her a place to live. She would not cost much, and she would make few demands. . . .

He broke the thought as she came toward him, setting the cup before him and then slipping into the chair across the table.

"Thanks, Doc."

He was startled. "For what?"

"For putting up with me last night. I don't feel sorry for me much. I know what I am. I know my place and I don't often get out of it. I shouldn't have said what I did."

"What was that?"

"The way you look at Mrs. Collins. It's not my business and I don't blame you. I think she's wonderful. I think she's about the nicest person I've ever known."

Mary Collins appeared to attract praise from everyone. It was not merely that she had volunteered to come to this mountain pesthole and nurse the sick. Rather they all seemed to recognize instinctively that she did not sit in censure on them, that she did not feel degraded by association with them.

"She is," he said. "Now, shall we forget it? There's still work to do."

It snowed again during that night. It snowed intermittently during the next three days, but Adam Patch hardly noticed. He was busy, fighting for Clint Collins' life.

Surprisingly the big man was rational. Most of the others, including Sam Dohne, remained unconscious from the first. But the second day, Collins greeted Patch with a scowl and no words. Apparently the fever had not changed his attitude toward the doctor. He seemed to mend, but by the third day, he was clutching desperately at any hope in his fear of death.

It came at three o'clock the following morning. Kid Beale brought the news, rousing Patch, who had gone to bed only an hour before. He had not undressed, and he rose and followed the gunman hurriedly up the rut of the snow path and into the hospital.

Mary Collins and Lily were at the rear of the room, working over a patient who had just been brought in. She did not turn as Patch approached Collins' bed, tested for a pulse and for breathing and, finding none, motioned silently to Kid Beale.

The gunman and his assistant lifted the body and slipped quietly out. Patch walked to Mary's side then.

"We did all we could, Mary. You must

understand that."

"I'm all right." Her voice was steady, even, without inflection.

"Of course," he said. "Go to the hotel now and sleep."

"I'll be better to be busy. I wouldn't sleep in any case."

He looked at her carefully, then said to Lily, "You go then. You'll be needed later on."

She nodded and went quietly out, leaving them alone except for the patients, all of whom were either unconscious or asleep.

Mary Collins drew a long breath. "Well, it's over."

"I'm sorry, Mary."

"I know." She was silent for a moment. "I did give him a little while. I paid him back a little for what he did for me."

"You paid him a great deal even before he became sick. You have nothing to regret."

"It's strange," she said. "I didn't love him, not in the way people are supposed to love. I guess I rather mothered him. He was a little boy."

Patch knew that she was talking more to herself than to him and he stayed silent.

"That's why he went to pieces. He never really quite grew up." She looked at Adam as if for confirmation. "It wasn't that he was a coward. He wasn't a coward."

He had turned and started toward the medicine shelf when Lindsay Stewart hurried into the room.

"I just heard."

Patch motioned to him. "Leave her alone."

Stewart looked at him hard.

"Sometimes it's better for people to be left alone for a little while. She has a readjustment to make. I don't care what she thought of Collins; death is always a blow when it comes to someone who has been close to you."

The lawyer hesitated, then nodded.

"Give her a little time. She knows how you feel about her. Don't rush her."

"You think I have a chance?" Lindsay Stewart sounded more meek than Patch had thought possible.

"I don't know." Patch was tempted to say, "Do you think I have?" He didn't. He had never been a man who shared his emotions. Aloud, he said, "I'll leave you in charge while I catch some sleep."

He was doing something which he greatly regretted doing, leaving them alone together at this moment. For grief is not predictable, and she might turn to the lawyer for comfort now.

He did not sleep. He lay wrapped in the

131

blankets, wondering why he should worry about the future when it seemed that there might be little future for any of them, and finally, at noon, he could stand the bed no longer. He rose, dressed and went down to eat.

Afterward he walked the well-beaten path through the deep drifts to the store. There were fewer than fifteen people in the cluttered room. With the deaths and the recent desertions, the population was noticeably smaller.

He did not linger, but went on to the hospital, wondering how many had died while he had been gone. He came into the quiet interior to find Lily Meyer and Annie Lee alone. Both had been crying and he guessed at once the cause.

"When did Maggy die?"

"An hour ago. They just took her away." It was Lily who answered.

He walked on, toward the medicine shelf and the charts. Then he stopped. Sam Dohne was sitting up in his bed. For a moment he thought the man was delirious, and turned quickly toward him. Then he saw that the beady eyes were rational, and said:

"You'd better lie down."

"I beat it, Doc." Dohne's voice was weak but steady. "I beat it. Old Sam Dohne. He's too tough to die."

"Lie down."

The mineowner obeyed reluctantly. Adam Patch took his pulse, his temperature, pulled back one eyelid and then the other. The whites had a yellow cast but the skin had lost its angry flush.

"I guess you're right, Sam."

Dohne nodded. "They been trying to kill me one way or another for years, Doc. They just ain't strong enough to wipe old Sam out." He was silent, wondering on it. Then he said in a different tone, "They tell me Clint's gone."

Patch nodded.

"And Maggy."

Again the nod.

The man sighed deeply. "That leaves me."

Patch said, "If you're talking about that gold ball, don't forget that Clint has a wife, and maybe Maggy has some heirs."

Dohne thought this over and some of the pleasure drained from his face.

"Mary's entitled, I guess. But you won't find no one to claim Maggy's part." He cackled.

"I wouldn't be too sure," said Patch. "People have claimed kinship to people lower than Maggy when money was involved." He walked back to Lily.

133

"How long ago did Mrs. Collins leave?"

"About three hours."

"All right," he said. "Hold the fort a little longer. I'll be back."

He went out and down to the hotel again. There was no one in the lobby but he heard sounds from the kitchen and followed them in search of coffee.

Lindsay Stewart was seated at the table, a steaming cup before him, talking to the cook. He looked up as Patch came in. The doctor picked up a clean cup, filled it at the stove and came on to the table.

"How was Mary?"

"All right. She's taking it well. She's in her room asleep."

Patch hoped that he was right. "Maggy South left us."

Stewart shrugged. "She made a lot of men happy, give her that."

"I liked her."

"For what she was, she wasn't bad." There was an intolerance in Stewart's voice which Patch had noted there before. He changed the subject.

"Sam Dohne's going to make it."

Stewart's mouth was cynical. "The good die young."

"Collins?"

Stewart shrugged. "I had nothing against

him except for Mary."

"Speaking of Mary, I had to remind Sam that Clint left a widow. He'd already decided that the gold ball belonged entirely to him."

"That," said Lindsay Stewart softly, "is one piece of thievery that Mr. Sam Dohne is not going to get away with."

Patch felt a growing warmth in his stomach. Certainly the coffee seemed to be heating him.

He said, "I left the two girls alone at the hospital. I'd better get back there. When Mary wakes, tell her we won't need her tonight."

Outside, it seemed to have grown colder and he snuggled his chin down into the upturned collar of his coat, ducking his head against the blast.

The heat in his stomach changed to a pain, as if the coffee he had drunk had settled there as a hot solid, but despite the warmth, he shivered, and before he had traveled a hundred feet there was a sudden dull ache at the base of his skull.

He suspected then and tried to hurry, to reach the hospital before the unconsciousness he had seen in so many others would strike him down. He failed to make it by two hundred feet. A sharp pain lanced between his temples, seeming to pierce his brain like an arrow. He went to his knees, his legs suddenly too weak to hold him, and with his hands deep in the chilling snow he crawled another twenty feet before he went forward onto his face.

Lily Meyer found him ten minutes later. One of the miners in the hospital had died and she was on her too-frequent search for Kid Beale.

She stopped, staring, and then ran to the store, screaming the news before she reached the closed door, bursting in with hysterical cries.

The men piled out and came up the street at a half run, both those who had had the fever and those who had not. They formed a silent circle around Adam Patch, staring down at him, hardly believing what they saw.

Patch had seemed invulnerable. Patch had given them courage by his presence, re-assurance that they needed. Then Kid Beale pushed his way through the circle and, gathering the unconscious doctor into his arms, carried him up the street.

CHAPTER TWELVE

Lindsay Stewart woke Mary Collins as soon as he heard the word, and she had never seen him as upset as he was in this moment.

"Patch is down."

"The fever?"

He nodded. "They found him in the road, in the snow. I'd been talking to him right in the hotel kitchen only a few minutes before." He pulled a handkerchief from his pocket and wiped his forehead although it was chilly in the room. "You'd better come. Lily and that other girl have completely lost their heads. No one seems to know what to do."

She said, "As soon as I can dress —" and he stepped from the room, closing the door behind him. Mary Collins lay for a full minute without moving. She said to herself in the half darkness, "No. This can't happen. It can't. Not two in twenty-four hours. I couldn't take that, Lord."

She sat up then, shocked at what her subconscious had betrayed her into saying. "I must be losing my mind. I barely know him."

But as she dressed, she remembered a hundred tiny things about Adam Patch. His gentleness with the sick, the way he smiled at her. The cold mask of his gambler's face which failed somehow to conceal the inner warmth.

She stood beside his bed looking down at

the face which was already flushed and turning the angry, magenta-purple, and knew a wave of terrible, dry nausea.

Never since she had been very small had Mary Collins been entirely at a loss. She had the independence which the Irish have treasured for a thousand years, a fierce inner pride that seldom admits defeat, and she was at her best when confronted by a crisis.

But she had not the slightest idea of what to do now. She went through the motions of undressing him, and by her quiet efficiency, her steady self-control, she calmed the two girls far more effectively than she could have done with words.

They came to help her as she stripped the clothes from the strong, muscular body. They bathed him with cool wet cloths, trying to quell the intense fever now consuming him.

Patch lay motionless, not stirring save for the short, labored breaths, rough and rasping as a file on hard metal.

For twenty-four hours Mary Collins did not leave the hospital. Then Stewart forced her to go to bed, pointing out that if she collapsed, there would be no one left who knew what should be done.

The weather cleared again, and almost all

of the die-hards decided at last to make a dash for the camp at the bottom of the canyon. Even the glittering presence of the gold ball no longer had the power to hold them. With Patch sick, apparently dying, they lost what little nerve remained to them.

Only Kid Beale and a half-a-dozen of his close friends remained. They stood on the store porch surrounding the ball of gold and watched scornfully as the departing citizens straggled down the canyon on their makeshift snowshoes.

Lindsay Stewart was inside the deserted building, watching the exodus through the dirty window. His attention was as much on Kid Beale as on the decamping train, and his shrewd eyes were thoughtful.

Sam Dohne was recovering from the fever but he was still in bed, still too weak to assert authority. Patch was unconscious, and the lawyer with his practical mind had already written him off.

That left Beale, his friends, Stewart and the women. The three girls he cared nothing about. To his way of thinking nothing could happen to them that had not happened already many times.

It was Mary Collins he was thinking about. He had seen the way Kid Beale watched her, and he was not fooled by the small kindnesses performed by the outlaw during the epidemic.

Basically Kid Beale was utterly ruthless, and since Stewart was consciously ruthless himself, he recognized the quality in others. He knew that he had little chance of standing against Beale alone. While the others had been here, there had been the possibility of rallying support if it were needed, but with everyone gone except this crew, there was no place to turn for help.

He considered killing Beale at once, and the reactions which would be generated. He had no more compunction against the thought than if Beale were a mad dog in his pathway.

But he decided against it, for the likelihood was that some of Beale's friends would manage to get him in return, and then Mary would be even worse off.

Beale finally shrugged and came into the store, and Stewart noted the abrupt change in his manner. There was a touch of swagger, a trace of arrogance normal to the man but which had been missing ever since Stewart had arrived at the camp.

The man walked around the counter to the whiskey barrel and deliberately filled half-a-dozen cups, passing them out to his followers. Lastly he turned, extending a cup to Stewart, his cold eyes now mocking.

"Join us, Counselor."

It was a direct challenge, a flaunting of the rule Adam Patch had laid down, a dare to Stewart to pick up the challenge or admit that Kid Beale was running the town. Stewart's smooth, handsome, boyish face showed absolutely no expression. He had stood before too many judges, played with too many juries to be out-thought by a ruffian like Beale.

"Why, thank you," he said, and advancing, took the proffered cup and downed it in a gulp.

Some of the tension that had been building up within the store lessened, for Stewart calmly walked around the counter, filled his cup and drained it a second time.

Kid Beale said in a different tone, "You aren't afraid of the fever, are you?"

Stewart looked at him deliberately. "Why should I be? A man only dies once. Whether I die here or somewhere else is not too important."

"I've had the stuff," said Beale. "The rest of these boys had it in Tonopah. But you haven't. Why didn't you go down the trail with the rest?"

"Maybe I like it here."

Beale laughed. "No one likes it in Gopher.

No one ever did. Maybe you're interested in that ball sitting out on the porch?"

"It could be."

"Because we're going to take it with us as soon as we figure we can get out. And no one is going to stop us. No one."

"Why should I try? It's nothing to me, I don't own any part of it."

"But Mary Collins does."

They stared at each other and Lindsay Stewart sensed for the first time why Kid Beale was really dangerous. The man had the killer's urge. It was buried deep inside him, carefully masked by his cold exterior, but now it glowed in his eyes. He had restrained himself for a long while, but now it was breaking through.

Stewart said evenly, "I've heard that you're good with a gun. I'm not bad myself. Shall we try it?"

The words caught Beale off balance. The urgency in his eyes grew. Stewart went on, utterly unconcerned.

"Or shall we postpone the heroics? That ball of gold that seems to interest you so much won't do you a lot of good if you're dead."

Beale laughed suddenly. "No one ever talked like this to me before."

"No," said Stewart, "because everyone's

always been afraid of you."

He turned away unconcernedly, walked to the counter, chose a cigar from an open box and lighted it, letting the smoke drift up between them.

"You and I are very much alike, my friend. We take what we want and we don't care too much how we get it. So why should we fight as long as we don't get in each other's way? You walk on your side of the street and I'll walk on mine. When they try you for murder, look me up." He turned on his heel, slowly, and slowly walked out of the store, leaving nothing but silence behind him.

In the hospital he found Annie Lee, Lily Meyer and the third girl whose name he did not know. He said,

"Most of the men just pulled out. The cook from the hotel went with them. Which of you knows how to use a skillet?"

The third girl said, "Me."

"All right. What's your name?"

"Jane."

"Supper at six, then, Jane." He looked at the others. "How's Patch?"

Lily's voice broke in a choke. "He's no better. He just lies there and his breathing is worse, as if his heart was up in his throat astrangling him."

Stewart went to the bed and looked down

at the unconscious man. He knew a certain regret. He had respected Patch as he had respected few men. The doctor had a solid strength and a basic goodness without being prissy. He lived in the world and understood the world and was a little cynical about both it and himself.

Stewart had small use for professional do-gooders and he had been suspicious of Patch until he realized that the other was a man first, a doctor second. Too bad, he thought, that Patch should have come up here to sacrifice himself for a bunch of bastards who would be better off dead.

But that was the way of the world, and Lindsay Stewart also had long since accepted the world, evaluated it and made his own peace with the pattern.

He backed away, almost bumping into Lily who had moved up beside him.

"You think he's going to die?" Her voice still had the curious break and Stewart looked at her, raising his eyebrow.

"A lot of people have died. What's one more or less to you?"

"He isn't one more or less." A fierce note rode into the voice to kill the quaver. "He's the doc. He's the greatest man I've ever known."

Stewart lowered his head forward. "And

how long has this been going on?"

"What's been going on?" She was beginning to get angry. "There's nothing going on. It's just that he treated me like a human, not like dirt. You wouldn't understand that, would you, Mr. Lindsay Stewart? I remember you. You came to our place at Tonopah. The high and mighty gentleman, that's what you were. You should hear some of the things the girls told about you."

Stewart struck her across the face. There was a red spot of anger in each of his cheeks. As she jerked back he spun and stalked from the room. Going down the snow-clogged street, shoulder-deep now in drifts, he fought for control of himself.

He swung into the hotel and stopped, finding Mary in the lobby looking fresh from her rest. The surge of his need of her swept up through him.

She said at once, "You've been to the hospital. How is the doctor?"

"No change."

He saw the hope fade from her face and guessed for the first time that Adam Patch meant more to her than just the man who had cared for her husband. And he knew the first touch of jealousy and put it aside, trying to laugh at himself for being jealous of someone who was nearly dead.

145

But it showed him something that he did not like. If he did marry her, he would probably be jealous of every man she smiled at, no matter who he was.

He said, "There's other news." He tried to keep his tone light, unaffected. "Our population has shrunk." He told her of the exodus, he told her of Kid Beale's taking over, he told her how Beale had disregarded orders and passed out the whiskey to his men.

"This changes things," he said. "I have a small gun in my room. I'd rather you did not go on the street alone, especially at night. But if you must, carry the gun and do not hesitate to use it."

She stared at him. "Kid Beale has never been anything but courteous to me."

"You're a woman," he said roughly. "You know how he has looked at you."

Color touched her cheeks.

"And things are different. For some reason Beale seemed afraid of Sam Dohne. Sam's up and around, but he has no strength, and whiskey makes men do things they might not otherwise try."

"All right," she nodded. "Get me the gun."

He moved quickly back along the hall. When he returned, he heard her voice in the kitchen, talking to Jane. He went through the door, paused there as the two women discussed the evening meal. Then Mary turned to him and he handed her the little weapon.

"You know how to use it?"

She looked down at the small pearl-handled piece of wickedness, noting the fine workmanship, the scrolled barrel.

"You like nice things."

"Beautiful things," he corrected her, and saw her color deepen as she understood his meaning. "We'd better be getting to the hospital."

He nodded, and taking her arm led her from the building.

CHAPTER THIRTEEN

It snowed. All during the night and all the next day. By the time the storm stopped, all marks of the retreat down the canyon had been wiped out.

Adam Patch remained in coma. Mary Collins insisted upon staying within call around the clock. To this end she directed Lindsay Stewart to curtain off one corner of the hospital room with blankets, and to move one of the beds behind this screen.

The lawyer would have protested more vigorously but for the conditions in the camp. Thoroughly snowbound, the outlaws had established themselves in the store, ignoring Sam Dohne's protests, and were managing to keep themselves continuously drunk.

Dohne hardly left the hotel. Gradually he was regaining his strength, but Beale had taken possession of all the guns save the one Stewart wore and the little one which the girl kept hidden in her dress.

The work at the hospital lightened. No new cases appeared. The group with Beale had already survived the fever and neither Stewart nor any of the women showed signs of catching it.

Three more men died and Scarface Boyer surprised everyone by waking one morning, calmly climbing out of bed, finding his clothes and staggering down the street to join the roisterers in the store.

Adam Patch remained as the only patient on the third day, and no one was ever watched over more carefully than he. Stewart thought sourly that it was a shame the doctor was not conscious to realize the attention lavished upon him.

He left the hospital and plowed through the waist-deep snow. With so few people left in town there was no longer need for the death cart, and the track was not well broken without its passage. He came into the hotel doorway from the brightness outside, and paused to allow his eyes to adjust to the indoor gloom.

Kid Beale's voice said, "You are not very careful, Counselor. Put your hands up."

Stewart turned towards the sound. Beale was seated in one of the lobby chairs which he had pulled to the right of the entrance. The heavy forty-five, which he held as if it were a feather, pointed directly at Stewart's middle. Slowly Lindsay Stewart raised his hands.

Beale said in a conversational tone, "I actually hate to do this. I really like you. Maybe that's why I am doing it. It would have been easy to kill you, but I won't. I'll just take your gun."

Stewart did not answer.

"Turn around, lean forward and put your hands against the wall."

Stewart obeyed. He felt the lessened weight as the gun was lifted from his holster. Then he heard Beale say,

"We've searched your room and Patch's. No guns. I guess this takes care of things."

The door behind Stewart opened, then closed. He took his hands from the wall and straightened slowly. He was shaking a little, not from fear but from inner tension. He knew that he had escaped death by a minor miracle. For some reason Beale's natural desire to kill had not shown itself. He crossed and sank into Beale's chair, considering the best thing to do.

There was no question that Beale was in control of the camp. By disarming Stewart, he had removed the last possible resistance. Yet there was still the gun that Stewart had given to Mary Collins. The logical way out of the situation was to retrieve the gun from her, watch his chance and kill the outlaw.

He rose, having made his decision, and left the hotel, walking slowly back toward the hospital, conscious that men were grouped on the store porch and that they watched him. He searched his mind for the excuse he would give the girl for asking for the return of the gun, for he could not tell her what he intended doing.

But as he entered the hospital he had no chance to say anything. Lily raced toward the doorway as he came in, her eyes shining.

"He's better. He's better."

For the moment, Stewart had no idea whom she was talking about; then he saw Mary Collins and the other girl beside Patch's bed. The doctor's eyes were open and Stewart saw that the man was rational.

He said automatically,

"This is wonderful," and wondered at the relief in his own tone. A few moments before he had felt utterly alone, cornered by Beale's wolves, forced to make whatever decisions were to be made. Now he had Adam Patch. Lindsay Stewart had never been one to depend on others for his decisions, and it puzzled him, his sudden willingness to shift the responsibility to Patch.

The doctor's voice was weak and had a faraway, hollow sound as if he were speaking through a long, echoing tube.

"Hello, Stewart. How's it going?"

Mary Collins said quickly, "Everything is fine." She threw Stewart a warning glance. "We haven't had a new case in days. I think we've finally beaten it."

Patch closed his eyes. He was asleep, but even to Stewart's untrained eyes there was a difference. The raspy breathing had softened, become less labored, the face had lost its flush and was now very pale.

He stood looking down at the man and then raised his eyes to Mary Collins' face. She was not looking at him. Instead, her full attention was on Patch. Stewart said in a low tone,

"How long ago did he come to?"

"Just before you came in. I was standing here and his eyes opened suddenly, and he spoke my name."

"You think he's better?"

She nodded.

"I hope so."

"He is. I've seen others come out of it the same way. Mr. Dohne, that scar-faced man . . . their fever breaks and they are rational. They're weak, but it's surprising that they come back so quickly. We've got to watch him now, to keep him warm. We certainly don't want him dying of pneumonia."

Mary Collins was right. Two days later, Adam Patch was able to walk the length of the bleak room and on the third, he insisted on being moved back to the hotel.

In all of his life Adam Patch had never spent one full day in bed before. Despite his training he had an impatience with illness when related to himself, and he brushed aside Mary Collins' urgings that he conserve his strength.

It was warmer in the hotel lobby. The potbellied stove glowed a cherry-red in its corner and sounds came from the kitchen where the three girls had established themselves as cooks. The door opened, admitting wind and snow, for the white fall had begun again that morning, and Sam Dohne came in.

Dohne had not fully recovered from his bout with the fever but his heavy face was red from the wind and his eyes swollen. He stomped the snow from his feet, opened his thick coat and crossed to warm his raw hands at the fire.

"Will it ever quit this damn snowing?"

Patch said nothing and Dohne looked at him.

"What's eating you, Doc?"

"Nothing." Patch had been sitting there thinking of Stewart and Mary Collins who were up at the hospital gathering the medicines and supplies to move them back to the hotel. He wondered what was taking them so long.

Dohne grunted. "I was just down at the store. They threw me out."

Patch turned his head. "Threw you out? Who threw you out?"

"Kid Beale and his crowd. Don't you know about them taking over? Hasn't anyone told you?"

"Told me what?"

"Soon as you went down, the rest of the bunch got scared and took off, and Beale declared himself boss. He got my guns and he got Stewart's and yours and he and his gang have been loafing around the store guzzling whiskey and eating all the supplies. They're just waiting for a break in the weather to try to get out with my ball of gold."

The man sounded near tears. Patch laughed.

"You know, Sam, this amuses me. You've been a thief all your life. You've stolen from everyone you ever came into contact with. The Gopher mine is probably the first halfway honest effort you've made. And you struck it a lot richer than you deserve. So, if someone is going to take it away from you, I couldn't care less. You know now how it feels to be robbed."

"Maybe you don't care about my share of that gold, but what about Mrs. Collins'? Don't forget Clint had a big interest in the mine."

Patch's eyes narrowed on him.

"And you'd better believe that Beale is aiming to grab it all."

"So let them take it." Mary Collins had opened the outer door in time to hear the last words. "I told you yesterday, Sam Dohne, that I didn't want Adam bothered about these things."

Stewart followed her in, carrying a box of medicines. He set it on the floor beside the wall and closed the door, then he turned around.

"Yes, Sam. If you know what's good for your hide you'll let them have the gold and forget the whole business. Beale would rather kill you than look at you."

Dohne was fuming. "A fine thing, when a man can't protect his own property."

Patch spoke from his chair. "And just how do they expect to transport it anyway?"

"They've built a sled," Dohne said. "It's got a cradle in the middle. They plan to force their way down to the wagon camp, grab one of the wagons and all the horses, and head south for the border."

"I don't envy them the trip." It was Stewart. He walked to the dining-room door. "What's for dinner?"

The next day, Patch ventured outside and the following day walked down as far as the store. He could feel strength returning to his legs, and he had always held the theory that the sooner a patient could be gotten on his feet the better off he would be. It seemed to work, for although he took his time and kept close to the line of roofed porches fronting the deserted buildings he gained the store without much sense of fatigue.

The first thing he saw was the sled. It was

155

a crude affair but effective, mounted on iron runners, a round hole in its top. Above it, on the porch, sat the gold ball like a huge Christmas-tree ornament draped in snow. He looked at it for a long minute, thoughtfully, thinking of what it represented in the way of labor, in the way of men's desires.

From within the building he heard the raucous sound of drunken laughter which even the thick door and double windows did not drown. He mounted the snow-packed steps and pushed the door inward.

Inside the store was a shambles. They had shoved the counters away from one corner and there made beds, piling up blankets from the stock, one on another until each man had a thick, mattresslike pad. A stove had been carted in from one of the other buildings and a man stood before it stirring what appeared to be a great pot of stew. Dirty glasses lined the counter around the whiskey keg, and one man slept in the middle of the floor before the doorway, his drunken snores adding to the confusion of four or five voices.

The voices ceased as Patch opened the door. Even the man at the stove stopped stirring, and every eye turned on the door.

Patch stepped in. He walked forward, stepping deliberately over the sleeping drunk. Kid Beale was seated on the counter beside the whiskey barrel, a half-full glass in his hand.

He looked up and his voice was mocking, with none of the respect in it that he had showed when the fever was raging.

"Hi, Doc. Something we can do for you?"

"Yes," said Patch. "A drink."

Beale showed his surprise. He sat for a moment motionless, then he picked up an empty glass, wiped it with a dirty rag from the counter and half-filled it, extending it watchfully.

"I thought you were opposed to drinking."

"That," said Patch, "was during the sickness. No one ever accused any Patch of not liking whiskey."

Beale laughed. "Your old man could never be accused of it, that's for certain. Have another."

He took the glass and refilled it. "You know, Doc, I was beginning to think that being a sawbones had turned you soft."

Patch did not answer.

"I suppose you've heard that we're taking the gold ball?"

"That's Sam Dohne's problem."

"I thought maybe you'd figure to play the gentleman and take the widow's side."

"Lindsay Stewart's the only gentleman I

know of in this camp. I'm shanty Irish from all I can find out."

Beale laughed again. He was a little drunk. "I always said your old man was a bigger thief than I am. I guess maybe you are too. This doctor business fools me. The only sawbones I've known were drunks or pious as a preacher."

"I'm neither."

"So, we don't want trouble. Come two warm days so this snow will pack a little and we'll be on our way. Right now it's fluffy as flour, a man would have a time trying to cart that chunk of gold out of here now."

"Think you'll make Mexico?"

"Tell me why not?"

"I'll not try to tell you anything. It's a long way, and when you get there some Mexican may have golden dreams of his own."

"Don't worry. I got friends below the border. I'll send word we're coming. We'll have enough company that not even the rurales will want to touch us. Have another drink, Doc. You sure you wouldn't like to come with us?"

"What a man likes and what he does are not always the same thing." Patch extended his glass. "Just one more. My head isn't as solid as it usually is."

Chapter Fourteen

For half of another week the three men and four women at the hotel sat and watched and waited. After Patch's visit, no one ventured in the direction of the store. It was like two camps, watchful of each other, squatting in the isolation of the snow-choked canyon, wary and uncertain.

Sam Dohne grew more dour with each passing hour, Lindsay Stewart more silent, the three girls increasingly nervous as they wondered about their own fate. Without Maggy to tell them what to do, they were lost and leaderless.

Lily stayed as close to Patch as she could, seldom speaking, seldom taking her doe eyes from his face. Her attention made him uneasy but he did not know how to escape it without hurting her and this he refused to do.

At night, alone in his room with a wall so thin that he could hear Mary Collins as she stirred in her hard bed, he lay awake wondering what her plans were, what the future might hold for any of them. He had no doubt that Stewart had already asked her to marry him, and under normal circumstances, Patch would have thought this an ideal match for her. The lawyer could give her far more of the material things than she had ever had. He could show her the world and help her to appreciate what she saw.

But there was something about Stewart that bothered Patch, something elusive on which he could not put his finger. The man, he felt, was hesitant and indecisive. It was a facet he had not observed in Goldfield. There Stewart had seemed so coldly certain, dominant without being aggressive, possessing the sure, calm confidence which comes with utter self-control.

But now he seemed on the defensive, especially with the women. It was almost as if he avoided Mary Collins purposely, and he was openly rude to the three girls, apparently resenting their presence in the hotel.

Adam Patch was still thinking about it in the morning when he came into the dining room and found Stewart alone at the table. The lawyer looked up and nodded without speaking. There were dark circles beneath his eyes and a nervous twitch jerked at a muscle in his delicate cheek.

Patch eyed him without appearing to. Lily came from the kitchen and set a plate of side meat and beans before Stewart, and smiled shyly at Patch.

"Good morning."

He said, "Good morning."

The girl returned to the kitchen and got Patch's breakfast. She put it in front of him and then, after an instant's hesitation, she pulled out the next chair and sat down.

Stewart looked up suddenly, sharp irritation in his voice. "Get the hell out of here."

Lily's head came up quickly, her eyes startled. Then color climbed into her cheeks, two tears came as if squeezed from a tube and ran down the soft curve of her young cheeks. She shoved back her chair, but Patch caught her arm.

His voice was raw with swift anger. "What do you mean by that?"

Stewart turned to him and his own face was a mask of cold fury.

"She knows better than to sit down with decent people. Why does she stay here anyway? Why doesn't she take the other girls down to the store crowd where they belong? Maybe they could get part of that gold."

"She stays here," said Patch, "as long as she wants to."

The girl moved convulsively. Patch did not release his grasp.

"Then I'll find some other place for Mrs. Collins."

"I think you'll find that Mrs. Collins does not share your intolerance."

Stewart stared at him for a long moment

of unbroken silence. Then he rose and stalked into the lobby and they heard the outer door slam behind him. Patch let go his grip on the girl's arm. She was shaking and he told her in a soft voice:

"Forget it. People like Stewart aren't worth being upset about."

"He's right. We shouldn't be here."

"Who's to say who should be where? You don't think you're actually disturbing Mrs. Collins by your presence?"

"Well," she was trying to think things out. "I guess not. Only, well, she's not like other people."

"She has some common sense," said Patch. "It makes her very different from the run-of-the-mill human being. She takes situations as they are and makes the best of them. She's not like Stewart, setting himself up in judgment of social morals and actions."

"He hates us." The girl said it vehemently.

"Hates you?" Patch raised an eyebrow. "What are you talking about?"

"He does. There are men like that. They . . . they aren't satisfied to be only with a nice woman. So they come to us, and then they are ashamed of themselves."

"Lily. Forget what happened here. Go on back to the kitchen and finish up. I judge

Mrs. Collins hasn't come down to breakfast yet?"

"I peeked in her room. She said she had a headache, so I got her some tea."

He nodded. "Go on back and see if she's awake, see if she wants me to check on her headache."

The girl went away. Patch searched his pockets for a cigar and failed to find one. He sat waiting, turning over in his mind Lily's comment on Stewart.

Lily came back to say that Mary was awake, and he moved on down the hall to find her in bed, her head propped up by two pillows.

He said, "This headache. You aren't by any chance coming down with the fever?"

"I don't think so." She gave him a small smile. "It's much better now since Lily gave me the tea."

He took her pulse and her temperature. There were none of the signs that he had learned to associate with the presence of the epidemic, and relief came to him.

"When Lily said you were sick I was afraid it was going to start all over again."

"So was she. That's the first thing she asked when I said my head ached. She's a good person, Adam."

Patch shrugged.

"What are you going to do about her?"

He showed his surprise. "What am I . . . ? Nothing that I know of, why?"

"She's in love with you. She'd do anything you asked her to. You could help her, Adam, if you would, and she needs help badly."

"Look," he said. "I have no desire to play God. It is dangerous to play with people's lives, Mary. Lily will have to find her own way if it is to mean anything to her."

"It's not like you to be hard."

"You know very little about me. I have the reputation of a gambler. I drink too much. I consort with characters who are disapproved of by the better elements."

"You're making fun of me."

"A little, yes. But I was raised to believe that every man should look out for himself and that you should not interfere unless help is asked."

She said, "If Clint Collins had felt that way about it when he first found me I have no idea what would have happened. But I probably would have wound up as Lily has. You don't mind if I help her, do you?"

"Why should I mind?"

She bit her lip and color rose into her cheeks. Why indeed should he mind about anything she did? It had been a slip, an unconscious admitting to herself that

Patch's opinion of her actions was important to her. She watched him go, thinking about it carefully, thinking about Stewart, thinking about marriage.

She was a woman who should be married. She recognized this about herself. Some women had very little need for a man, merely using them toward their own ends. But with her, it was different. She needed marriage not so much for security as for companionship.

She had never made friends easily. There was a shyness about her which made her hold a little apart except during emergency. But she needed someone with whom she could talk freely.

This she had had with her first husband, but never with Clint Collins. And this she had found again with Adam Patch.

She was easy in his presence. She was not easy with Stewart. She had always been on her guard with him, but she had attributed it to her embarrassment that he should attempt to make her leave Clint.

Now with Clint dead, his behavior puzzled her. At first she had supposed that he avoided her out of consideration for her widowhood, but his behavior had become more and more noticeable.

She sighed. She pushed back the blankets

and shivered as her bare feet touched the cold boards of the floor. If the snow would only let up. If only they could return to Goldfield. She dressed slowly and then went out into the lobby.

Neither Patch nor Stewart were in sight. She went on to the kitchen to find Lily washing dishes, Annie drying them.

"Where did the doctor go?"

"Back out to the hospital. There were still some things left there."

"What things?"

They did not know.

She hesitated, then went back to her room for her coat and stepped out into the deep snow of the street. The sun was bright, the sky clear, and she became aware suddenly that it was far warmer than it had been in days. Little edges of moisture glistened on the building fronts at the top of the snow. It was actually melting, and the air had a softness that it had lacked before.

The knowledge brought a quick wave of relief and she was humming to herself as she turned toward the lodge hall. But she had traveled less than fifty feet when Kid Beale swung out of what had been the blacksmith shop.

She stopped, not knowing what to do. She saw at once that he had been drinking, but he did not seem to be drunk and his tone was clear when he said,

"I was just coming to the hotel to get you."

"To get me?" Panic welled up in her and she felt in the pocket of her coat for the gun. It was not there. "What do you want with me?"

"We're pulling out."

"I don't understand."

"You will. You're going along."

"Now wait just one minute."

"You wait." Beale's voice was cold and metallic. "You're going with us. If you give us no trouble, you won't get hurt. I got a lot of respect for you, Mrs. Collins, more than I have for most women. Generally they aren't honest, but you are. You don't primp and pose and try to make men notice you. I've had bad luck with women."

She gaped at him, startled.

"But don't think I'm going soft. We're taking that hunk of gold and we mean to get it clear to Mexico."

"But what has that to do with me?"

"We don't want people following us. Patch and Stewart have both fallen for you. They don't want you hurt."

"So?"

"So if we take you along, they'll think twice before they try to stop us. Because

167

I'm going to tell them exactly what will happen to you if I'm followed. Come on."

He reached out to take her arm. She tried to pull away.

"Look," he said, "I'm trying to be nice. Do you want Patch and Stewart shot?"

"Of course not."

"Then come along quietly. If we have any trouble, the simple thing is to shoot them."

She stared at him, only half believing. "You would do that?"

"Why not?"

"I can't understand you. All during the fever you were so helpful. I liked you. I found it very hard to believe a lot of the stories I'd heard about you."

"They're true."

"Then why did you help so during the fever?"

He rubbed the side of his stubbled jaw with the edge of his thumb. "You got me," he said. "It never occurred to me not to help."

CHAPTER FIFTEEN

Adam Patch returned from the hospital carrying the case of surgical tools that Stewart had forgotten. He saw the men grouped around the sled at the store porch and knew a sense of relief for he realized that the waiting was over.

He quickened his step slightly, and then he saw Mary Collins and began to run. He dropped the instrument case beside the hotel porch and plowed through the thick snow, making frustratingly slow time.

He was panting heavily by the time he reached the group.

Kid Beale was holding the girl by her arm with his left hand. His right was free, hanging not far from the gun at his hip. He turned as Patch came up, and the men around the sled turned.

Patch's eyes sought the girl's face, then between gasps for breath he said to Beale,

"What's the idea?"

"Simple," said the outlaw. "Just a little insurance, Doc. As long as neither you nor Stewart or Dohne try to follow us, she'll be all right. If we have trouble she gets hurt."

Patch shook his head. "I can't speak for Dohne, but certainly I'm not going to chase after that gold ball, and I'm pretty sure Stewart isn't."

"See that you don't."

Adam Patch knew a complete helplessness. He knew that nothing he could say or do would change Kid Beale's resolve in the least. Nothing short of violence would stop the outlaw, and his chance for violence was slim indeed. Not only had he not recovered his full strength but he had no gun, and he was up against seven men, men as tough as any in that part of the country.

Only a fool would go against such odds, and Adam Patch was not a fool. In his own right he was as cool a gambler as had ever hit the mining camps.

Had he thought it would do any good he would have rushed Beale then and there, hoping to catch the man off guard, to grab him, probably to snatch the gun from the holster.

But the odds against success were very large. He would manage only to get himself killed and, dead, he could do nothing for Mary Collins or for anyone else.

He said tonelessly, "You win."

"Now that's sensible, Doc. I told the boys you were grown up. It's Stewart I'm afraid of. I know the breed. I come from Virginia myself. These gentlemen are damn fools when they think their honor is involved."

Under other circumstances, Patch would have laughed. The description of Stewart was so accurate. But he found nothing laughable in what was happening here. He turned and walked away, conscious that Mary Collins' eyes followed him, conscious that he was failing her in a moment when she needed help as she had never before needed it.

He sat down on a corner of the store porch. His knees were as weak as if they were joined the wrong way. The late morning sun was warm on his back. The snow around him was melting slowly. The air felt like spring. It was the season of the year which brings the beginnings of life.

And he must sit here utterly helpless.

He hated Kid Beale suddenly, hated him as he had never dreamed that he could hate. He felt that he could tear the man's throat apart with his bare hands. If something happened to the girl. . . .

They were loading the sled, rolling the sluggish ball of gold carefully from its long-occupied perch into the cradle waiting to receive it. When it was solidly in place, it was securely tied with ropes. And two of the men caught up the sled rope and plodded down the street.

Behind them from the hotel came an agonized roar and Sam Dohne galloped through the hindering snow in his shirt-sleeves.

Beale yelled at him to stop. But it was as if Dohne had gone deaf, as if his rage at seeing his fortune hauled away had unhinged his mind. He charged the group bare-handed, like a bull that has been tormented past the point of reason.

They scattered like startled quail. One man went down, then a second, but as Dohne turned in search of more victims Scarface Boyer brought the barrel of his rifle down across the mineowner's head with a sharp cracking sound that made Adam Patch wince.

Sam Dohne fell, going flat on his face to lie motionless in the trampled snow. Mary Collins had been standing silent, watching the action. She started forward instinctively toward the dropped man.

Beale jerked her back. He turned her around and said something in a voice so low that Patch could not hear, then he marched her down the street, the girl awkward, unaccustomed to her snowshoes.

Patch continued to sit, to watch. One of Beale's men remained beside the porch, his rifle at ready. He waited until the party had reached the foot of the twisting street, then went after them.

Patch stood up. He walked across and rolled Sam Dohne onto his back so that the man would not smother. Dohne stirred and groaned. The snow beneath his head was red from the gash which the rifle's sight had dug across his scalp.

Slowly he sat up, to Patch's amazement. The doctor would not have been surprised if Dohne had never sat up again. The blow had been sufficiently vicious to have killed him.

"You've got a hard head."

Dohne sat fingering it tenderly as if to make certain that all the pieces of his skull were still in place. Then, wobbling, he got to his feet and staggered into the empty store.

Patch followed and found him at the whiskey barrel. He drew a cup of the brown liquid and poured it down his throat, then he drew a second and afterward a third.

Patch said, "That won't help."

"Damn them. God damn them." Dohne hurled the cup clear across the store. He was actually crying.

Patch left him there. He figured that the mineowner would drink himself into a stupor and go to sleep. At least Patch would not have to worry about him for a little while.

At the hotel he found the three frightened girls huddled in the lobby. Lily said in a desperate voice:

"They took Mrs. Collins. You let them take Mrs. Collins."

Patch crowded down his hot reaction. "What did you expect me to do, play the fool like Sam Dohne and get my head bashed in? Would that have helped?"

Lily began to cry. "I didn't mean that. I'm sorry I said it, only when I think of Mrs. Collins with those terrible drunken beasts. . . ."

Patch didn't like the thought either. "Where's Stewart? Do any of you know?"

"I saw him climbing toward the mine." It was Annie Lee.

"The mine? What did he go up there for?"

"I don't know."

Patch went back to the street. He climbed to the turn-off which led up to the mine road and there saw the tracks of Stewart's snowshoes in the deep snow. He hesitated. There was nothing much the lawyer could do and Patch was turning away when he glanced upward and saw Stewart come around a bend in the trail. He waited as the man floundered down to him.

"What are you doing up here?"

"Looking at the mine. I figured that if Sam took out that much gold, the vein should be worth seeing."

"Beale and his men pulled out."

"With the gold?"

"And with Mary Collins."

"Mary?" Stewart had started to move past Patch. He stopped.

"They took her along as a hostage, to keep us from trying to stop them."

The lawyer was swearing in a tight voice. "I'll kill Beale. I'll kill him. I meant to do it tonight."

"And just what are you going to kill him with, your hands?"

For answer Stewart pulled a small gun from his vest pocket.

Patch frowned suddenly. "Where did that come from? I thought Beale had taken all of yours."

"I gave it to Mary for her protection. After he took my other gun, I stole it back from her."

"You stole it? Why? Wouldn't she have returned it to you?"

"Of course, but she'd have worried if she'd known how I intended to use it. How long have they been gone?"

"Half, three-quarters of an hour."

"All right, we can catch them easily. They can't move too fast dragging that sled."

Patch shook his head. "You've got that popgun, they've got seven rifles and they have the girl. Beale said that he'd kill her if we tried to follow. I, for one, believe him."

Stewart looked at him helplessly. "But

we've got to do something. Where are they headed?"

"Mexico."

Stewart's brows came down. "They really are? It will take them three weeks. How far does Beale intend to take Mary, all the way?"

"He didn't say." Patch turned and headed again down the street. For once in his life he found it hard to make a decision. The best he could think of was to wait until the outlaws had progressed so far that they would not think they were being followed, then make his way down the canyon and out to the Tonopah road.

Once he could get to Tonopah or Goldfield he could alert the country to the south by telegraph. But that country contained some of the most barren land in the United States and Beale had undoubtedly already chosen a route which would be hard to follow.

They came into camp in time to see Sam Dohne emerge from the store. He carried a bundle under his arm. He had put on a coat but his head was bare and the heavy hair was matted with drying blood. Stewart gasped.

"What happened to him?"

"He tried to stop them and they clobbered him with a rifle barrel."

Dohne swung his head at the sound of their voices, then he stepped down into the snow, saying in a thick voice,

"I'll make them sorry, the thieves."

"Sure," said Stewart, "you'll make them sorry. How?"

"With these." The man reached into the bundle and brought out a stick of dynamite. To it he had attached a short length of fuse.

Patch swore softly. "You damn fool, you'll kill Mrs. Collins too."

"That's her lookout. Nobody pushes Sam Dohne around. Nobody." He was very drunk, so drunk that he staggered as he walked, but not drunk enough to fail to carry out his threat.

"Now wait a minute, Sam." Patch took half a step forward. "Don't be a fool. Just cool down a little until we think of some sensible way to stop them. We'll get your gold back."

"Stay where you are." Dohne had dropped his bundle into the snow and pulled a match from his pocket. "You're not going to stop me, Doc. No one's going to stop me. Just don't try, or I'll blow your head off."

Patch stopped. Behind him, Stewart quietly drew the small gun from his pocket. He was partly masked from the bigger man by Patch and he raised the weapon before

Dohne realized that he was armed.

"Put it down, Sam. Slow."

The big man hesitated. He stood undecided and Stewart told him in a quiet voice,

"Put it down or I'll kill you."

Dohne moved suddenly. He side-stepped in an effort to further screen himself by Patch's body, at the same time lighting the match with his thumbnail and holding the small flame to the end of the fuse.

Stewart shot him twice, once through the body, the second bullet striking him full in the face. As he fell, he flipped the dynamite directly at Patch.

Adam's hand came up instinctively to catch it. He hurled it away instantly, dropping as he did so, shouting at Stewart to follow his example.

Stewart threw himself headlong across Patch's legs as the stick exploded, throwing up a geyser of snow, the noise of the explosion echoing and re-echoing from the canyon walls.

For a full minute Adam lay where he was, then he came slowly to his knees and afterward to his feet. He moved over as Stewart rose and looked down at Sam Dohne.

Dohne had cheated death so many times that men said that he bore a charmed life.

But this time the magic had failed to work. Stewart's bullets had accomplished what the Kansas rope and Soapy Smith's toughs had failed to do, they had cut down one of the most unsavory characters to ever grace the frontier.

Stewart did not even trouble to look at the body. He thrust the small gun in his coat pocket, went around the corner of the store, got the death cart which Beale and his helpers had used and brought it back to the street.

Together they raised Dohne's body to the cart and wheeled it with difficulty through the impeding snow to the crevasse which served as the common grave.

They walked back to the store in silence. Neither man was affected by what had just happened. Dohne was not the first man that Stewart had killed, and Adam Patch had come as close to death half a dozen times before. As they reached the spot where Dohne had fallen, Stewart stopped and picked up the bundled dynamite.

He stood staring at it thoughtfully as if an idea were forming in his razor-sharp brain.

"You know, maybe Sam had something at that."

Patch stared at him in surprise.

"We might be able to bluff Beale with this. Of course we couldn't actually use it with Mary around, but we might get him to turn her loose if we promised to let them go on with that silly ball of gold."

"You're out of your mind. Beale knows we wouldn't use it. He'd merely shoot us as soon as we got within rifle range."

"Not if we came up to them in the dark, and it will be dark in a couple of hours."

"It still won't work. Beale is no fool."

"You forget," said Lindsay Stewart, "I am a lawyer. I am used to convincing juries, which is the same as saying that I can convince people.

"Beale knows me. He knows that I am interested in Mary Collins, but he also knows that I am as cold-blooded and calculating as he is. He will believe that I would kill her rather than have her shared by seven men."

Patch stared at him. "I believe you would kill her under the circumstances."

"I would," said Stewart. "I'd blow everyone off the map rather than have Beale's dirty hands on her, but I won't have to. Wait and see. He'll believe me."

"All right," said Adam. "It's worth a try. I can't think of anything else to do. I guess Mary would rather be dead at that."

Chapter Sixteen

There was no moon. A storm was blowing up from the west, and black clouds had already blotted out most of the stars, like a creeping tide swallowing a sandy beach.

But as most snow does, the white blanket beneath their feet gave out a certain luminescence that made it possible for Patch and Stewart to follow the broken tracks after darkness closed in around them.

They had left the town two hours before, leaving the three frightened girls as its sole occupants. Patch had assured them that they would be all right. There was nothing to fear save loneliness. There was plenty of food, plenty of wood, and he would send a rescue party back for them as soon as possible.

He and Stewart moved down the twisting canyon in single file, their homemade snowshoes made walking difficult and their progress was agonizing in its slowness.

They had been on the trail an hour when the tracks they followed turned into a side canyon which led upward in a series of switchbacks to the distant rim.

Why Beale had chosen this route rather than following the main canyon had puzzled Patch at first, but as they climbed, the snow thinned, and he realized that the outlaw must have guessed that the wind which had drifted the white substance into the canyon until it was twenty- or thirty-feet deep in spots, would have cleared the upper rim.

At the top, the path turned eastward and their progress quickened as the snow beneath their feet thinned, occasionally showing the seamy face of the bare rock.

But the climb up the canyon side had taken most of Patch's strength and he realized that he was not as recovered as he had thought. Finally against his will he was forced to rest.

He sat, his back to the trunk of a wind-twisted tree, wondering how much farther they would have to go before they caught the men with the gold sled.

Stewart had not sat down. He paced about, saying nothing but showing his lack of patience in his constant movement.

After five minutes, Patch rose and they took up their chase. Now Stewart was in the lead with Patch trying to keep up. He slipped and stumbled with increasing frequency on the slippery path. Finally Stewart stopped and waited for him to come up.

"You've just about had it." There was no sympathy in the lawyer's tone. It was merely a statement of fact. "Sit down and rest awhile. I'll go on alone and you can catch up when you feel like it."

There was the stubbornness of an Irish bulldog in Adam Patch.

"I'm all right. Just keep going."

Stewart looked at him keenly. Then he drew a flat bottle from his pocket. "I filled this while you were at the hotel."

Patch accepted the bottle. The raw whiskey ran down through him, restoring his faltering circulation, easing the slight sickness at the pit of his stomach which told of exhaustion. He drank again, and then returned the bottle.

Stewart had his drink, then corked it carefully and returned it to his pocket. He watched without comment as Patch rose slowly and the march continued.

The trail veered away from the canyon rim as they reached a deep gully that couldn't be crossed and made a wide, looping detour. Suddenly Stewart stopped, staring across the side canyon.

Patch turned his head. On the far side, screened by the dwarf timber, he caught the glint of firelight. It was like a shot in the arm. The weariness which had drugged his mind slipped away, and his legs seemed to grow a new strength as they moved forward, cautious now along the looping trail, keeping in the shadow of the trees as nearly as possible until the trail dipped, crossed the side canyon and swung back northward.

As near as Patch could judge, they were within half a mile of the little campfire. He called to Stewart softly.

"They've stopped. Half an hour won't make much difference. Give me that much time to rest."

The lawyer came back to him as Patch, not waiting for an answer, slumped gratefully to the snow-covered earth. He sank down beside him and pulled the bottle from his pocket.

The liquor warmed Adam as nothing ever had and he realized that he had been nearly freezing without being conscious of the cold.

Stewart drank in silence, deliberately corked the bottle before he said, "I'll go on alone. If I get Mary free, I'll send her back along the trail to you."

Adam started to protest, but Stewart cut him short.

"There's nothing you can do to help. They either buy my bluff or they shoot me. What's the sense in both of us getting shot?"

He uncorked the bottle again and passed it to Adam.

Patch drank. He was beginning to feel

nearly normal. Stewart finished the bottle and laid it reluctantly on the ground. He took the small gun from his pocket, found a box of shells and extended them to Patch.

"If they shoot me, see what you can do with this." He rose. Without waiting for Patch's answer he turned and moved away through the quiet night.

Patch sat where he was, fingering the gun. He broke it, checked the bullets, then got up slowly and moved along the path after Stewart.

He went slowly, conserving his strength, not knowing what he would run afoul of. And suddenly in the brush ahead of him, he heard Stewart's voice lifted through the night.

"Beale, Kid Beale. Can you hear me? This is Lindsay Stewart."

Adam Patch had stopped unconsciously. He listened, staring through the mat of trees at the distant fire, waiting for movement. Then he heard Stewart's voice again.

"What's the matter, Beale? Are you too sleepy or too scared to answer?"

"I never was afraid of anyone." It was Beale. He had stepped forward, so that he was outlined in the firelight. It was a gesture of contempt, even though he thought that Stewart was entirely unarmed.

"I warned you not to follow us. No one is going to take this gold."

"Who wants the gold." Stewart had also moved and Patch could see his dark form now, crouched behind some low bushes between him and the fire. "Let the girl walk over here and I promise you that you and your men can take the gold to hell or any place else you choose."

Patch had started to move forward slowly again. He was within a hundred yards of Stewart when Beale laughed.

"Think I'm a fool? If you had the girl safe, you'd raise the country against me the minute you got safely back to Goldfield. You won't, my friend, because you love her. You both do, you and Patch. I've watched you and I know. You will do nothing to jeopardize her safety. Therefore I keep her with us as insurance."

"And what happens to her? Think what this trip will do to her."

Beale was unmoved. "I'm sorry, but that's the way it is. Go while you can."

"All right," said Lindsay Stewart, and there was a cold finality in his voice which raised the short hairs at the base of Patch's neck.

"I've got half a dozen sticks of dynamite. You've got three minutes to send the girl over here or I'll blow the whole world to hell."

He held the stick up in the light. He scratched a match and the tiny flame lent substance to his words.

There was a sudden stir around the fire as men scrambled to their feet. Beale sounded incredulous, a little shaken.

"You wouldn't kill her."

"Rather than let her go to Mexico with you, sure. You've got two minutes."

And then Adam Patch saw the shadow move between him and Stewart. He opened his mouth to shout his warning, but he was too late. He saw the muzzle flare of the rifle before he heard the shot.

Lindsay Stewart went down without a sound and a man's exultant cry rang out through the night. "I got him. I got the bastard." He moved forward to stand above his fallen victim, his rifle held at the ready for the finishing shot if it were needed.

There was confusion from the camp, and under the blanket of noise that Beale's men were making, Adam Patch was running forward, the small gun clutched in his fist. He was within ten feet of the murderer before the man heard him. The man swung around, bringing up his rifle, but he was too late. Adam Patch shot him full in the face.

He saw the man fall but he had no interest in him as an individual. He wanted the rifle, and the short gun on the belt around the waist.

He ripped it free, not stopping to fasten it about his own hips. There was not time, for the men from the camp were already crashing through the brush.

He caught up the rifle with his other hand and dived back into the shelter of the trees. He was not a moment too soon for bullets were already searching the timber for him. He ran south from the trail, away from the edge of the side canyon. He did not want to be hemmed in against the rim.

The ground rose steeply, the sharp rocks hidden beneath their cover of snow.

He tripped and fell, and he kicked his snowshoes away. It was impossible to run wearing them, and he had to run.

The sound of the men's pursuit was very close. He scrambled to his feet and went upward. Fortunately the wind had shifted most of the snow covering from the mountain side. It was only halfway to his boot tops.

His breath was short, his chest felt as if it were locked in an encircling iron, but he labored on silently, finally finding a sheltered nook behind two rocks which rose like giant teeth before the sheer wall which marked the mountain's face.

He dropped into it in near-exhaustion and lay for a few minutes without moving. Then he straightened and peered between the rocks at the slope up which he had just traveled.

Nothing moved on its bare whiteness, but below, in the thicker timber, he could hear the sound of the men's voices as they pressed forward and knew that it would be only a matter of minutes before they found his tracks.

He could not stay where he was. The face at his back could not be climbed. He was in a trap as certainly as if the nook had been baited with cheese.

He crouched there, debating, and then he saw the first man come from the timber, point to his tracks and heard his excited shout. He was joined by a second, and then a third man.

In the uncertain light, they were little more than shadowed shapes and it was impossible to pick out Kid Beale or to be certain that the outlaw was in the group. And then Adam Patch heard his voice, coming plainly through the chill air of the night.

"Why'd you have to follow us, Doc? Why

couldn't you have let things alone?"

Patch didn't answer.

"We know you're up there. We can dig you out if we have to, but you'll only get killed and none of the boys want that. They like you, Doc."

Still no answer. Patch felt the rifle as his hands tensed and he laid the barrel along the rock. He wished that he could be sure which of the shadows was Kid Beale. Even in the uncertain light he felt that he had a better than even chance to hit the outlaw.

With Beale out of the play, the others might turn and run for it with the gold, ignoring the girl. He did not know, but it was worth a try.

But until he was sure he did not want to waste ammunition. There were four shells in the gun and still six men against him.

He eased up to his knees for a better look, but the shapes at the edge of the trees were too blurred for him to see clearly.

And suddenly there was excitement below. A man came running out of the timber, shouting Beale's name.

"She got away. She's loose. She's hiding somewhere and I can't find her."

The group broke up, turning, running back into the timber until they disappeared from sight.

CHAPTER SEVENTEEN

Patch knew it might be a trick, an effort to draw him from his hiding place. But he had nothing to lose. At daylight they could dig him out of his place behind the rocks. Far better to come out now and take his chances. If Mary had escaped he might be able to distract their attention long enough to permit her to get away.

He eased around the rocks, grateful for the small rest that had been granted him. He moved cautiously down the hill, his eyes studying the line of trees. He caught a sign of movement just before the shot, and dropped flat, waiting until he saw the flare of the gun in the darkness.

His returning shot brought a cry of pain out of the blackness, and he heard the thrashing in the brush as the man fell.

There was no second shot. He rose carefully and made the trees without incident. Apparently only one man had been left to watch for him. He worked through the brush, finally stumbling across the body. The man was dead. There was a belt half filled with rifle shells about his middle.

Gratefully Patch transferred some of them to the belt he had taken from the other outlaw, reloaded his rifle and moved forward through the trees.

He stopped from time to time, listening, but heard nothing. Ahead of him the small fire still made its tiny light, a beacon toward which he moved silent as a shadow. He heard someone in the brush to his right, and paused, and heard the man curse as he apparently fell over a rock.

There was a streak of light on the east. Dawn was not too far away. He had no plan, all he hoped to do was to distract their attention so that the girl might make good her escape. Suddenly what he had taken to be a tree was a man, a man whose rifle was pointed at his head.

"Hold up. Who is it?"

Patch shot him. The sound of the rifle was whiplike in the night. He did not wait to see whether the man was dead. He turned and ran, tumbling into a snowbank which had formed in the shelter of a rock reef, clawing out. The shot would bring the searchers hurrying back toward camp.

Three down. He wiped the snow from his face and finding the shelter of a large tree, crouched behind it waiting. Three down, four men still on their feet, four men hunting him, hunting Mary, and the light in the east was growing fast.

He waited, then he heard Kid Beale's

voice, off to the right, near the rim of the side canyon. "Who shot? Answer me. Who shot?"

There was no reply. He heard Beale swear. "Boyer, where are you?"

A voice answered from beyond Patch.

"Any sign of the girl?"

"None."

"That damn doctor is loose somewhere. I should have killed both him and Stewart before we pulled out. Watch yourself. It will be daylight soon."

Patch was very conscious of the growing light. The world was no longer black, but a dull gray. He dared not wait much longer. He moved toward the sound of Beale's voice.

The light grew. Time was running out. He had to find Beale. He had to settle with Beale before the others saw him, before the chance was lost.

And then they came face to face. Beale stepped into the small clearing from the north just as Patch emerged from the timber.

They stopped. They stood motionless, looking at each other like two wild animals who have met by chance at the same water hole.

They were about fifteen feet apart. Both

were carrying rifles, both had revolvers in their belts, but neither made any move for a full minute. Then Beale said, "Well, Doc?"

It was a question, unhurried, unexcited. Kid Beale had many faults, but cowardice was not one of them, and he had been in situations like this before.

Patch said, "Put down your guns, call your men, get your gold and get out of here. All I want is the girl."

"I can't trust you, Doc. I've got to kill you."

He brought up the rifle in a swinging arc. But he was not fast enough. Patch shot him twice. The reflex action of death tightened Beale's finger on the trigger and his rifle exploded as he fell, the bullet kicking up loose snow at Patch's feet.

There was a crashing in the brush behind Patch and someone jumped on his back before he could turn, carrying him to the ground. He twisted, but his attacker had been joined by a second and then a third man.

They hauled him to his feet, pulled the gun from his belt and spun him around. Scarface Boyer said, "You raised hell, now didn't you, Doc. You surely raised hell."

Adam Patch did not answer.

Boyer considered him. "You know, Doc.

You saved my life. Not that it's worth very much but for some reason I'm kind of fond of living. There's places and things I ain't seen yet. I hate to kill you. I really, truly do."

One of the other men laughed. "You sound real sweet, Scarface. Why not kiss him and be done with it."

Boyer swung the butt of his rifle up and clipped the man neatly on the jaw. The man went down cursing. The third man stood looking on, uncaring.

Boyer said, "You never did have much sense, Bert. If we didn't need you to help haul that damn sled I'd put a bullet in your stomach."

He looked at Patch. "If I thought you'd throw in with us, I'd let you take Beale's place. We need another hand. But the trouble is you got principles. I had a partner who had principles once, and what did it get him? — a rope."

Patch said, "I'm making the same offer to you I made to Beale. Take your gold ball and go. I haven't any interest in it. All I'm concerned about is Mrs. Collins' safety."

"She won't get hurt." Boyer sounded sincere. "After what that girl did at Gopher I'd walk over hot coals for her. Beale, he had ideas. That's why I ain't sorry that he's

195

dead, because if he'd laid a hand on her I'd have had to kill him."

"Then take the gold and go."

"Can't do it, Doc. Can't take the chance. I know you mean the best in the world, but we can't take a chance on you talking. Come with us and it's a deal."

"He doesn't have to go with you." It was Mary Collins. She stood behind them, in the edge of the timber, the rifle that she held covering them carefully.

"Drop the guns, Boyer."

The man hesitated. Her rifle exploded, the bullet going over their heads. "The next one will be lower." Her tone was as collected as if she were discussing the weather. "I mean it."

He let the guns drop. Patch disarmed the other two men.

Boyer said in a plaintive voice, "You took advantage, ma'am. If you'd been a man I'd have made a try for it."

"You'd have been a fool," she told him. "Anyone could have killed you as you turned." She had come forward. Patch could feel pride for her rise up through him. She was entirely self-controlled, utterly at ease.

"Where were you?"

She gave him a faint smile. "I was never

more than a hundred yards from the camp. There's a hollow tree and I crawled into the trunk. I didn't come out until I heard you talking. Then I found the man you shot and got his rifle."

"Lucky for me you did." He watched Boyer as he talked, debating in his mind what he would do with the prisoners. Even disarmed, they presented a threat.

He could shoot them. He was not a sentimental man. In the circumstances Lindsay Stewart would have. . . .

And then he thought of something. These men had only one real interest. All they wanted was the gold.

Remove the temptation and he removed the danger. He said, "Let's go back to the camp," and turned, realizing that in the interval it had grown fully light.

The sled with its golden cargo rested beside the fire and Patch stared at the heavy ball, thinking of how much trouble it had brought them.

Gold had caused more grief in the world than any other single item. He said to Boyer, "Pull the sled over to the canyon rim."

They stared at him, not understanding, and he waved the rifle barrel suggestively. "Go ahead, or I'll put a bullet in your leg."

They watched him, studying him, trying to guess what was in his mind. Then, slowly, they picked up the ropes which were attached to the sled and pulled it toward the edge of the cliff.

The girl said, "What are you going to do?"

He gave her a faint grin. "Remove temptation."

Suddenly she understood.

"You're going to throw the ball of gold away."

"Maybe I should have asked you first. After all, a part of it belongs to you."

"I don't care. It isn't important."

"I thought you'd feel like that. We can always come back and get it after this is over, but I doubt that Boyer and the others can get it out of that canyon without equipment."

The men were staring at him. "You mean you're going to roll it down there, Doc?" Boyer sounded incredulous.

Patch sounded amused. He wished that Lindsay Stewart had lived to appreciate the joke. It was the kind of humor that the small lawyer would have understood perfectly.

"Tip the sled over, boys."

"Go to hell." Scarface Boyer had been spending his portion of the gold in his mind. To his way of thinking it was his, and he was not going to let it go without a fight.

Patch coolly put a bullet between his legs. It struck the sled and drew a long splinter from its side.

"Turn it over. Gold doesn't do a dead man any good."

Boyer was still defiant, but the other two ignored him. They stooped, caught the edge of the sled and raised it. The ball moved in its hole-like cradle, hesitated, then rolled from the sled across three feet of snowy ground, bounding down the steep, snow-covered slope as if it were made of rubber, to land with a crash, breaking the ice which bound the surface of the creek far below.

To Adam Patch, it brought an immense feeling of relief. Boyer was standing on the canyon rim, staring downward as if he had just lost the one thing which had made his life bearable.

He turned and walked away. Patch called after him. "If you can get it out of there, it's yours. We won't try to stop you. All we want is to be left alone."

The other two men shifted uneasily, then they started after Boyer, hurrying as they went. The girl sat down on the edge of the sled as if her knees would no longer support her, as if a delayed reaction had hit her suddenly.

"It's over."

"I guess so," said Adam Patch. "At least it will be when we get to the relief camp." He turned and walked back to the camp and threw some wood on the nearly burned-out fire.

"Is there food?"

She had risen and followed him. She nodded, pointing to a pile of sacks in the corner.

"Can you make some coffee? I'll go do something about Stewart." He moved away through the brush to find the lawyer's small body huddled where he had fallen, the stick of dynamite close by his fingers, the bundle to one side.

Patch hesitated. Burial would be difficult. The ground was frozen, and the soil thin at best. But he could not leave the body unprotected from prowling animals.

And then he thought of the hollow tree into which Mary Collins had crawled to hide. He could put Stewart in there, block the open end and send back for him from the relief camp.

He reached down and was startled to find that the body had not stiffened. Stewart was alive. He investigated quickly. The bullet had struck the small man in the upper leg, breaking the thighbone. The wonder was that it had not bled too freely.

He gathered him up in his arms and carried him back to camp. The girl was at the fire, frying salt meat in a blackened pan. She turned quickly and then gave a little cry.

"He's alive."

Patch nodded. "Get some blankets."

She spread the blankets on the ground and Adam laid the unconscious man upon them. When he straightened he saw the tears in her eyes.

"He means a lot to you, doesn't he, Mary?"

She said, slowly, "I suppose that any woman has a certain feeling for a man when she knows he loves her. He wouldn't be lying there if he had not tried to help me. Will he be all right?"

Patch said, "If we were in Goldfield I'd say yes without hesitation. Here, with the difficulty of getting him out, I don't know."

"The sled. Can we haul him on the sled?"

Patch nodded. "I'll get it."

"Wait. You haven't had any coffee yet." He turned quickly to the fire and poured a cup. He carried it with him as he went after the sled.

Five minutes later they were on the trail.

CHAPTER EIGHTEEN

It was nearly midnight when they came down the last grade and saw the fires of the wagon camp. Patch had never been so tired in his life and he knew that the girl must be near exhaustion, but there had not been one word of complaint from her.

He called, and saw a form throw back the blankets and rise, and he knew that it was Indian Jake.

At the moment he could have kissed the squaw man, he was so glad to see him. Instead he merely motioned to the still unconscious man on the sled.

"Make a bed for him in one of the wagons."

Jake looked at the lawyer. "Fever?"

"Bullet in his hip. We had a little trouble."

"Figured you had, when Boyer and those pals of his came busting down the trail this afternoon."

"Where'd they go?"

"Back up the main canyon. Most of the boys that were here went with them. The word got out you rolled that gold ball over the edge."

Adam Patch did not care who had gone after the gold ball. Tired as he was, he operated on Lindsay Stewart's thigh. He was afraid of gangrene. He dared not wait until he could get the wounded man to Goldfield.

It was an experience he would not soon forget. At least he had brought his small instrument case with him when they started after Beale.

Indian Jake held the lantern. Mary handed him what he required. The heavy rifle bullet had torn through the ligaments, shattering the bone and plowing on to come out the other side of the leg.

He made his preliminary examination, then opened the wound, removing the bone splinters and finally setting the leg. Lindsay Stewart would walk with a limp for the rest of his life, but at least he would walk.

He set the splints, washed his hands and turned back toward the fire. There were no people left in camp save the Indian packers. The men from Gopher had struggled up through the snow-choked canyon in their search for the gold ball.

The Indians sat beyond the fire, watching him wordlessly. He ignored them. He accepted a plate of food that Indian Jake set before him. Then he told the old man to harness the best team to one of the wagons and drive them to Goldfield.

Patch slept most of the way, balancing on the high seat beside the old man. Mary was asleep in the bed of the wagon beside Stewart.

They made twenty-five miles the first day and when they unharnessed for the night camp, Adam Patch felt as if he had returned from another world.

It was strange to be out of the snow. Strange not to have the feeling of constant pressure which had borne in on him all during the fever, stranger still to reach the Tonopah road and see the never-ending line of freight wagons as they hauled the supplies to the booming camp.

They came into Goldfield just at sunset. Stewart was conscious, weak, but his leg seemed to be healing cleanly. He smiled a little at Patch when the wagon pulled up before the entrance of the hotel, and two of the porters carried him inside and up to his third-floor room.

Their arrival created a sensation and, when Patch left the room after redressing Stewart's leg, he was forced to nearly fight his way through the lobby to gain the sidewalk.

Everyone had questions about the fever. He answered them as briefly as he could, finally escaped the crowd and made his way up the hill to the Collins' house.

There was a light on in the living room

and he heard Mary's step as he knocked.

"Who is it?" She had paused before drawing the bolt.

"Adam."

There was a moment of silence. Then she said, "Please, can't it wait until morning?"

He stared at the door. He had not expected this. "It can't," he said finally. "I was surprised when I came back down into the lobby that you had not waited until I took care of Stewart."

"I wanted a chance to think."

"Look," he said, and the impatience was plain in his voice. "It's not easy to talk through a closed door."

She opened the door, and he was shocked by her appearance. The tired lines were etched deeply at the corners of her eyes and mouth. He had not noticed them so plainly before. It was as if she had held herself under careful restraint all during the last few weeks, but, having returned to the safety of Goldfield, she was allowing herself to go to pieces.

It showed in her voice, in the way she moved nervously back across the room away from the door, and he guessed at a touch of hysteria and his conscience smote him for coming here tonight, but he knew a driving need to clear up several things.

"I'm very tired," she was almost pleading with him. "Please, Adam, can't we do our talking in the morning?"

He almost left then. Afterward he wished that he had, but instead he said, "I love you. I meant to tell you before, but there was not the chance."

She stopped her nervous pacing and turned back to face him. "Don't tell me tonight."

"Why not tonight?"

"Because it's too soon. Because you and I have been through a lot together in the last few days. I don't know, Adam. I don't think you know either."

"I know." There was deep conviction within him. He moved toward her. He took her shoulders in his powerful hands. "What's the matter? Is it Stewart?"

She shook her head. "I'm not going to marry Lindsay Stewart. That much I've decided, but I'm not certain that I will marry anyone else either."

She stepped back quickly out of his grasp, and he made no effort to stop her.

"In the name of God why?"

"I don't know that I can explain. I'm almost too tired to think. That's why I wanted you to wait until morning, because I'm afraid I might say something I don't

mean, because I might hurt you uninten-
tionally."

"You can't hurt me, Mary. I'm more
interested in your welfare, in your happiness, than I am in my own."

"I know, that's why I'm afraid of this,
Adam. At the moment you are feeling very
protective toward me. You saw me through
the trouble with Clint. You were with me
when he died, and you rescued me from
Beale."

"But —"

"Wait, please. I've seen other men become
protective toward women they have helped,
and I don't want you to mistake this for
love."

"I'm not — I —"

"Wait a little while. Wait until we forget
some of the things that happened to us in
Gopher. There are many things to consider.
You are Dr. Adam Patch. You are an important man in Goldfield. You have other
friends, other interests. You are too important to me for us to make a mistake."

"I don't know what you are talking about."

She sank down wearily on the couch,
conscious of her failure to get her point
across, yet wanting desperately for him to
understand.

"I've been married twice, Adam. I was not

in love with either of my husbands. I had something that they wanted and I figured that that was enough. But it isn't enough with you."

"Meaning that you do love me."

"Meaning that I don't know. I've got to be sure, and I've got to know that you are sure. What about Clara Holister?"

"It was a mistake —"

"You say that now because you've been with me. Let's be sure, let's not make a mistake. I couldn't bear for you to marry me and regret it later. Now, please, let's not talk any more tonight."

He walked down the crowded street, ignoring the restless people around him, his mind submerged by his own problems. The lights of the Northern laid their gay pattern across the sidewalk, and he turned in automatically as he had so many times in the past.

The room was crowded. It held the air of excitement that had always exhilarated him, for the Northern was more than a saloon. It was a social club, a second home for the lonely men who made up the bulk of Gold-field's population.

But Adam Patch got no lift from the throng tonight. Maybe he was tired, or maybe the last few weeks had altered his life and given it new purpose.

His experience during the fever had given him certain values which he had not realized before.

Rickard slapped him on the shoulder. "Just the man we were talking about, Doc. Do you think Boyer and his boys can get that gold ball out of the canyon?"

"Maybe, but that snow is deep and fluffy as feathers. Where'd you hear about it?"

"Indian Jake. The story is all over town. Everyone's laughing. You were a hero before. You're a bigger man now. It isn't everyone who would roll half a million dollars down a canyon side."

Wyatt Earp said in his quiet voice, "Who does it belong to? I've known Sam Dohne since Dodge, and I never heard anyone claim to be his relative."

Patch shrugged. Richard said, "Clint Collins owned an interest in that mine. Where is he?"

"Dead, the fever."

The gambler's eyes narrowed. "His wife, she went to Gopher with you. Indian Jake said you rescued her from Beale and his men."

Patch shrugged again. He had no desire to discuss Mary with these men.

"I'd say the gold belonged to her."

"I'd say so, yes."

"And she didn't object when you rolled it over the cliff. She must be some woman."

No, she had not objected. He had not given it much thought before. He had been too preoccupied with other things, but what right had he had to throw away a fortune for her? He did not know what her financial status was, but he could guess that Clint Collins had had little to leave beside his interest in the mine.

He turned and for the first time realized that the games around the pit had stopped and that the men in the saloon had crowded around him.

Everyone was interested in the gold. He saw the greed in their eyes and knew that before morning many of them would be headed for the mountains.

He answered their questions as best he could, and finally managed to break free, pleading weariness, and sought the peace of his father's drugstore.

But he found no peace. The lights in the front of the store were burning, but the door was locked. He used his key and stepped in, hearing voices from his own office at the rear.

He did not know who was with his father until he reached for the connecting door, then he stopped, feeling trapped, for Clara Holister was sitting in the chair beside his desk.

He heard his father say, waspishly, "Where have you been?"

He answered automatically. "At the Northern."

"I might have known." The girl had risen and he had a moment's realization of her beauty, and was ill at ease.

She was studying him, noting the thin drawness of his face, his sunken eyes, the three-day beard that still stubbled his cheeks.

"Things have been bad."

He nodded, not knowing what words to use.

"There are all kinds of stories going around town."

"I know."

"Are they true?"

He was not trying to evade. "I don't know which stories you mean."

Temper crept into her voice. "You might at least have come to the house. You might at least have saved my pride. My brother saw you going to the Collins' house."

He did not answer.

"I shouldn't have come here." Her anger was as much at herself as it was at him. "But

I had to know. I didn't want to make a mistake. I haven't, have I?"

He shook his head, silently. He had to admire her at the moment. She made no protest, there were no heroics.

"Good-by, Adam." She was moving toward the door. He did not answer and she was gone, and he knew that no matter what Mary Collins decided, one chapter of his life was closed.

His father was watching him with knowing eyes. "What's happened, Adam?"

Adam did not answer.

"It's that Collins woman. The whole camp is talking about the way she went to Gopher with you. What about her husband?"

"He died."

"So?"

"Look," said Adam Patch. "You don't understand."

"No one ever understands," said his father, "but let it go. I do not mean to pry."

Adam looked at him in astonishment. It was the first time in his memory that his father had not pried not only into Adam's business but into the businesses of everyone with whom he came in contact.

"Thank you."

"Sure," said James Patch. He reached under the counter and produced a half-filled bottle of elixir. "Have a drink."

Adam drank.

"Now go to bed."

Adam went to bed, but not to sleep. He twisted and turned until he had wrapped the blankets into a mummy-like case, but daylight came before he finally dozed off.

It was ten o'clock when he walked into Lindsay Stewart's room at the hotel. As soon as he came in, he realized that the small lawyer was better. Stewart was propped up with three pillows behind his head, freshly shaven, looking almost his normal self.

He gave Patch a small, shy smile as the doctor came in, saying with a trace of mockery, "I fooled you, Doc. Even your butchering can't kill a Stewart."

Patch did not answer. He took his pulse, then his temperature. "Don't get too gay," he told the smaller man as he shut his case. "By all the odds you should be lying in a hollow tree up above Mapse canyon."

"Hollow tree?"

"That's where I was going to bury you. It was the shock of my life to find that you were still breathing."

"I can imagine." Stewart's smile had grown to mocking. "With me out of the way, you'd have had her all to yourself."

Patch's face stiffened.

Stewart's voice turned bitter. "Don't worry about it. I'm not in the running."

Patch said, "I don't know what your talking about."

"Sure you do," said Lindsay Stewart. "I suspect you know too much. But I got up my courage this morning to ask her."

"This morning?"

"She came here to see me, to see how I was, to shave me, to nurse me. And I asked her to marry me and she wouldn't."

In spite of what Mary had said to him the previous night, Patch felt a certain quick relief. But it was short-lived, for Stewart went on. "She's going away."

"Going away, where?"

"To San Francisco, I think. She said that she might come back, later on, but she did not want you to know where she is."

"That doesn't make sense."

"I've found that few women make sense." Stewart shifted a little. "She is very Irish, my friend, and the Irish resent help, because they resent their need for help. You did your cause no good by throwing away her ball of gold. If she had that, she would be one of the wealthiest women in the country. She wouldn't feel that you were wanting to marry her merely to take care of her."

Patch stared at the lawyer.

"Maybe she'll marry you after awhile, after she's gotten a job and proved to herself and the world, and you that she doesn't need you. A woman hates to feel dependent upon a man. That's the mistake I made."

Patch found no answer.

"But I've learned something about myself and about love. Love should be unselfish. It isn't easy, but I actually hope that she does marry you because you could make her happy. I never could. Now get out of here. I hate the sight of you."

Adam Patch went. He felt very sorry for the lawyer, but he was far from happy himself. His impulse was to go and see Mary, but he realized that this would accomplish nothing.

But Stewart had given him an idea. If Mary were rich, if Mary did not feel that she needed his help . . . then . . . maybe. . . . There was only one way to make her rich, to recover the Gopher Gold.

Chapter Nineteen

The party that Patch formed for the recovery of the gold represented the leading citizens of Goldfield. It was headed by Bert Bell, the sheriff. It included Tex Rickard and Kid Highley and Wyatt Earp.

Adam knew that the remaining citizens of Gopher would not give up the ball without a fight, but he was certain that Earp's name was enough to throw fear into them.

A last-minute recruit was Patch's father. James Patrick drove out of Goldfield in a handsome buggy, following the line of horsemen as they took the Tonopah road.

There was a picniclike air about the operation. The thieves and the burglars who hoped to get a share of the gold for themselves had already headed for the canyon. They might fight it out with the men from Gopher if a showdown came, but they would not argue with men like Tex Rickard and Wyatt Earp and Adam Patch.

They made good time and they found the wagon camp still at the canyon's mouth when they rode in during the evening of the second day. It looked more like a small city than a camp, for at least two hundred men from Goldfield had arrived.

The canyon above was still choked with snow and had defied everyone's efforts to get through. Scarface Boyer was dead. Failing to get up the main canyon, he and his friends had returned to the side canyon, and he had attempted to descend the cliff by the aid of ropes. The rope had broken and he had fallen halfway down the canyon wall, landing against a tree trunk that jutted from the rock. His men reported that he had not moved.

It rained that night, packing the snow in the main canyon, and sending out a stream of water that forced the camp to move through the darkness to higher grounds.

By morning, the snow had packed until Patch deemed it safe to venture into the main canyon on snowshoes.

Indian Jake went with him. Rickard agreed to haul the sled back to the rim of the side canyon and to lower it to them on ropes. The rest stayed with the wagons, keeping an eye on the toughs who were growing restless under the delay.

They climbed in single file, the snow beneath their webbing settling into a solid block that was nearly ice. It varied in depth but Patch guessed that in places it was all of forty feet and he hoped that the pack would remain solid enough to allow them to drag out the sled.

By nightfall they had not yet reached the side-canyon's mouth. Indian Jake broke branches from one of the twisted trees that clung to the rocky slope, and Patch made coffee from melted snow as they munched cold biscuits and dried meat. Afterwards they slept wrapped in their blankets, their booted feet to the leaping fire.

Patch awoke at midnight, feeling moisture on his face and realized that it had started to rain again. He stirred, sat up and wearily climbed to his feet. Indian Jake with the instinct that had saved his life half a hundred times, was up at Patch's first move, reaching for his gun.

Patch reassured him. He gathered an armload of wood and dumped it on the dying fire, seeing the flames lick up at the dead branches.

The rain was heavier now and Jake grunted as Patch set the coffeepot on the blaze. "She come harder, we get a lot of water."

"It will have to rain a lot harder than this. That snow pack is fluffy as feathers. It'll soak up a lot." He sat down, draping the blanket across his shoulders and looked at the old man.

"You didn't have to come on this."

"I like her too."

Patch looked at him, sharply. "So you know what I'm doing this for."

"Sure. I know you aren't after that gold. You wouldn't have rolled it away in the first place if you'd cared."

"Think we can get it out?"

"If we find it."

"We should. Tex will be on the rim, and Boyer's body is still probably caught in the tree."

"A lot of snow."

Patch rose to pour the coffee. It was so hot that the rim of the tin cup burned his lips.

"Not as much as here. It crashed through the ice into the creek bed. The wind had cleaned the ice."

The old man merely shrugged. He had already used far more words than was his custom.

Patch said, "We can't sleep in this rain. We might as well push on." He finished the coffee, and wearing the blanket as a poncho started up the canyon. The surface snow was beginning to slush and he slipped on the ice beneath, but he kept going. It was daylight before they reached the entrance of the side canyon and turned into it. The rain had increased and they were soaked to the skin.

They stopped, making a small fire in a curve of the canyon wall and setting their coffee to boil. When the liquid was steaming in the tin cups, Patch laced it with whiskey from the bottle and passed it to the old man.

He was concerned about Jake, but he had to admit that the squaw man seemed to be standing up under the ordeal better than he was, for his teeth chattered as they touched the rim of the hot cup.

Then they were pressing onward. Jake was in the lead, muttering to himself. And now Patch had a new worry, for with the thinning snow they would have difficulty dragging the ball of gold out on the sled.

It was noon when they rounded a sharp curve in the canyon and saw the plume of smoke rising from the rim above them and realized that they were nearing the end of the trek.

Patch waved his arms and shouted, and saw Tex standing on the rim above him, and heard Rickard's words faintly through the steady beat of the rain.

"You'd better get out of there. This snow is beginning to melt. That canyon's going to be full of water before very long."

"I know it." Patch had been worrying about the same thing since morning. "Can you lower that sled?"

The sled came down, dangling above their heads at the end of the spliced ropes, and Patch turned back, moving along the creek.

The spot where the ball had fallen couldn't be more than a few yards in any direction, but the ice had frozen over it, and the rain had smoothed the ice's surface until the place where the ball had broken through no longer showed.

Adam finally picked up a club and went along the creek, breaking the heavy ice systematically. He was about to give up when Jake let out a yell behind him.

He turned back and caught the gleam of gold. The ball had nearly buried itself in a bar of sand, and the sand had washed over it until only a small portion showed.

Jake was already on his knees, scooping at the sand and Adam joined him, wondering as he did so how they would ever manage to lift it from the hole and roll it onto the sled.

Suddenly he heard excited shouts from above. He straightened. He could not understand what was being said, for the sound of the rain seemed to have increased until it was a roar.

And then it dawned on him that the roar was not the sound of the rain. He swung around to look up canyon. He saw it coming, the most frightening sight in the whole world, a thirty-foot-high wall of water roaring down upon them like an engulfing tidal wave.

He yelled to Jake. The old squaw man had

already seen it and was scrambling from the creek's bed. They ran toward the point where the rope which had lowered the sled still dangled along the canyon wall. Jake seized it and went up the face like a monkey on a stick.

Patch was slower, more awkward. He was conscious that Jake had reached a small ledge from which grew three small, wind-warped trees and was crouching there, reaching down toward him.

The flood struck. He felt the dashing water hit his legs, tearing at them like a thousand clutching hands. His fingers slipped on the wet rope, and for a moment he had the sickening feeling that he was about to be carried away; then Jake's clawing fingers fastened into the collar of his coat and he felt himself being dragged up onto the edge of the shelf.

He wrapped his arms about the trunk of one of the trees and realized that the old man was snubbing the rope around his body.

The water was still rising, its pounding waves coming up to his ankles, his knees, finally to his waist.

He glanced toward Jake. The old man was perched in the fork of a second tree, looking like a drowned scarecrow. The roar of the flood was deafening. The water threatened to tear the trees from their shallow-rooted moorings. The rope about his waist was the only reassuring thing, for the men above had pulled up the slack until it was taut.

He never saw the log which struck him. It was half rotten, having lain in the mountain meadow for many years before the flood water scooped it up and carried it down the canyon. Its softness probably saved his life, for had it been solid, the blow it struck him would have smashed his rope-held body.

As it was, the rotten wood broke as it struck him, but there was still sufficient force to crack the upper bone of his left arm and stove in three ribs.

He did not lose consciousness. He felt the stunning blow, the hot, knifelike thrust as his ribs cracked, and then the log veered off and went tumbling down the canyon's throat, half submerged in the raging flood, like a crocodile swimming with only its evil eyes above the surface.

He hung, limp, powerless to help himself. Had it not been for the rope about him he would have fallen back into the water.

They dragged him up, straining, lifting the rope hand over hand. The rope about his battered chest felt as if it were cutting him in two. His body bumped against the rock of the canyon wall.

But he moved upward, inch by painful inch until Tex caught him beneath the arms and dragged his body to the fire.

They had built a brush shelter against the rain, covering it with rubber tarps. A few minutes later, Indian Jake crept in beside him, curling up like a wet dog and going immediately to sleep.

They set his arm. Patch telling them what to do. They bound his body tightly to hold the cracked ribs in place, and then he slept, filled with hot coffee and whiskey.

When he awoke, the rain had stopped, the sun was shining, and patches of snow remained on the ground on the north side of the rock ledges.

Despite Tex's protest, Patch got to his feet and walked carefully to the canyon rim.

The flood had subsided, dropping almost as quickly as it had come up until it ran like a small river down the bottom of the canyon. But the bottom was no longer where it had been. A layer of mud, boulders and twisted trees, some twenty-feet thick hid the old stream bed. Adam Patch turned away. The Gopher Gold was as effectively buried as if a man had planned it carefully.

At his shoulder Tex said, "They'll probably never find it now. I wish I'd seen it, just once."

"They'll try," said Adam Patch. "There's nothing like lost treasure to drive men to insanity. They'll try, and maybe some day another flash flood will uncover it." He turned and walked painfully back to sit down beside the fire.

It took them three days to get him back to Goldfield.

He lay in his room above the drugstore and thought about the gold, and wondered what Mary Collins would do without it. His father kept him informed of the treasure hunt which was going on in the canyon. For men had not given up. They dug, they cleared a part of the old stream bed. They did not find the ball of gold.

Mary was gone. She had slipped out of Goldfield the day after Patch had started for the canyon, selling her house and all the furnishings. No one knew where she was. The stage agent only knew that she had purchased a ticket for Tonopah.

And then Adam heard her step upon the stairs. He thought that he would have known it anywhere. He had listened to it in the makeshift hospital at Gopher, in the hotel lobby and dining room.

He sat up quickly as she pushed open the

door. She stopped. She stared at him. She said, "You aren't dying."

"Dying. Would you like it better if I were?"

"Oh, Adam, no." She was in his arms, crying against the bandaged shoulder. He winced and she pulled quickly away. "I've hurt you."

"It's all right." He used his good arm to pull her back against him, to hold her thus while he kissed her. Finally she pulled away.

"What's this about my dying?"

"Lindsay Stewart wrote me. He said that you risked your life in a flood to get that stupid gold ball for me. I didn't want that gold ball."

"What did you want?"

She looked at him. She started to laugh, quietly, contentedly, a woman finally certain of herself. "You, I guess. I guess I have from the first night you came to the house."

CHAPTER TWENTY

They still call it Lost Gold Canyon, and a season seldom passes that some adventurous soul doesn't bend his back and pick at the dried mud of the old-time flood. Goldfield and its mines are little more than a memory. Tex Rickard, Wyatt Earp, Kid Highley are gone. But Dr. Adam Patch still

226

sits on his porch at Santa Monica and tells the story of the ball of Gopher Gold.

Most people don't believe him, but his great-grandchildren do, and one day, Adam the third plans to go into the mountains, and find the canyon. He does not know exactly where it is, maybe in Nevada, or maybe in California. The line is very close, and the country is rough, but he means to go. After all, the gold belonged to his great-grandmother; so why isn't it his?

ABOUT THE AUTHOR

Todhunter Ballard was born in Cleveland, Ohio. He graduated with a Bachelor's degree from Wilmington College in Ohio, having majored in mechanical engineering. His early years were spent working as an engineer before he began writing fiction for the magazine market. As W. T. Ballard he was one of the regular contributors to *Black Mask Magazine* along with Dashiell Hammett and Erie Stanley Gardner. Although Ballard published his first Western story in *Cowboy Stories* in 1936, the same year he married Phoebe Dwiggins, it wasn't until *Two-Edged Vengeance* (1951) that he produced his first Western novel. Ballard later claimed that Phoebe, following their marriage, had co-written most of his fiction with him, and perhaps this explains, in part, his memorable female characters. Ballard's Golden Age as a Western author came in the 1950s and extended to the early 1970s.

Incident at Sun Mountain (1952), *West of Quarantine* (1953), and *High Iron* (1953) are among his finest early historical titles, published by Houghton Mifflin. After numerous traditional Westerns for various publishers, Ballard returned to the historical novel in *Gold in California!* (1965) which earned him a Golden Spur Award from the Western Writers of America. It is a story set during the Gold Rush era of the 'Forty-Niners. However, an even more panoramic view of that same era is to be found in Ballard's *magnum opus, The Californian* (1971), with its contrasts between the *Californios* and the emigrant gold-seekers, and the building of a freight line to compete with Wells Fargo. It was in his historical fiction that Ballard made full use of his background in engineering combined with exhaustive historical research. However, these novels are also character-driven, gripping a reader from first page to last with their inherent drama and the spirit of adventure so true of those times.

We hope you have enjoyed this Large Print book. Other Thorndike, Wheeler, and Chivers Press Large Print books are available at your library or directly from the publishers.

For information about current and upcoming titles, please call or write, without obligation, to:

Publisher
Thorndike Press
295 Kennedy Memorial Drive
Waterville, ME 04901
Tel. (800) 223-1244

or visit our Web site at:

http://gale.cengage.com/thorndike

OR

Chivers Large Print
published by BBC Audiobooks Ltd
St James House, The Square
Lower Bristol Road
Bath BA2 3SB
England
Tel. +44(0) 800 136919
email: bbcaudiobooks@bbc.co.uk
www.bbcaudiobooks.co.uk

All our Large Print titles are designed for easy reading, and all our books are made to last.